OH, SALAAM!

OH, SALAAM!

BY NAJWA BARAKAT
TRANSLATED BY LUKE LEAFGREN

Interlink Books

An imprint of Interlink Publishing Group, Inc.
Northampton, Massachusetts

First published in 2015 by

INTERLINK BOOKS
An imprint of Interlink Publishing Group, Inc.
46 Crosby Street
Northampton, Massachusetts 01060
www.interlinkbooks.com

Library of Congress Cataloging-in-Publication Data
Barakat, Najwá.
[Ya Salam. English]
Oh, Salaam! / by Najwa Barakat ; translated by Luke Leafgren. --
First American edition.
    pages cm
ISBN 978-1-56656-992-7
I. Leafgren, Luke, translator. II. Title.
PJ7816.A6745Y3313 2014
892.7'36--dc23

                                2014032559

Printed and bound in the United States of America

General Editor: Michel Moushabeck
Editing: John Fiscella
Proofreading: Jennifer Staltare
Cover design: Pam Fontes-May
Layout design: Leyla Moushabeck
Cover art: Meryl Natow

To request our complete 48-page full-color catalog, please call us toll
free at 1-800-238-LINK, visit our website at www.interlinkbooks.com,
or send us an e-mail: info@interlinkbooks.com.

For all cities, like my own,
that have ever descended into madness.

Translator's note: *Salaam* is the Arabic word for "peace." The Arabic title, *Yaa salaam*, is both a way to address a woman by that name and a common phrase for expressing surprise, similar to "Oh, my goodness!"

CHAPTER 1

A cloud said, "Isn't this the city that no longer resembles itself?"

Another replied, "What's more, it's nothing like any other."

A third asked, "Is it true what they say about its people, that they never cry anymore?"

The teeming clouds jostled each other and crowded together, gazing down in amazement.

CHAPTER 2

The first light of dawn.

Luqman opened his eyes to the alarm clock. He didn't need it. Every day, just to spite it, Luqman would wake before the alarm by a few seconds, precisely at the time he wanted, just to show that he, Luqman, didn't need it.

Ever since Luqman had learned to make bombs, he had possessed an internal clock, razor sharp, that carved the flesh of sleep away from the bones of wakefulness precisely when he wanted. He took pride in it with his comrades. They would make bets with him, and he'd nail it. He always nailed it—times, locations, targets.

Truth be told, had Luqman been from any self-respecting country, he perhaps—no, he certainly—would have been made a general by now. Had the war continued, nourishing him with its blaze, his life wouldn't have shriveled up and blown away like ashes scattered in the wind. One day, all of a sudden and just like that, they had severed his war like a rope. Luqman's life tumbled backwards, head over heels, and landed in a heap. A coma, a paralysis of the brain—clearly Luqman's life was afflicted by something or other.

Luqman played with his penis. Come on, Partner, get up! I promise you a day unlike any other. He put his finger underneath to give it a boost, and "Partner" lifted its wobbly head. Then it collapsed back onto Luqman's belly and slept. It wasn't in the mood today. Oh, well. Luqman wasn't in the mood either. Maybe he would bring it to see Marina in the evening. Hadn't she begged him to come dozens of times?

Marina…God! When he first saw her, he was struck by how white she was. So tall and so white in the midst of this summer, a summer overcast but scorching, sticky and dusty, stinking with noxious odors, and crowded with dirty people and deafening car horns. Marina was amazing in the summer. And in the winter?…He didn't know. Cold and refreshing like a glass of soda, like a sweet scent with a touch of mint.

She had refreshed him at first sight. It was as though someone had stuck his head in a refrigerator and held it there, as though thousands of fans began dousing him with mild, autumnal breezes. Her legs bare, she danced like someone strolling along a secret tunnel carved through the disgusting heat of summer, slowly, leisurely, her dry skin never breaking a sweat. The swelter fell upon it and bounced away like a mirror reflecting light.

He had called her over to his table and opened a

bottle in her honor. She didn't smile, nor did she seem surprised; she had no reaction at all. Neutral, cold, gleaming—like snow.

The waiter said to him in Egyptian dialect, "First-rate Russian caviar! She arrived with last month's shipment. Seventeen years old! I swear to God, Mr. Luqman, you deserve an entire night with her. What do you think?" Then he turned to Marina and said in English, as he folded the fifty-dollar bill into a small pocket inside his jacket, "Marina, you can stay wiz Mister Luqman all ze nite."

Luqman hadn't intended to engage her for the whole night, especially when he remembered that the fifty was the last bit of money he had. But there was something in the tone of the waiter, who knew Luqman back in the days when dollars flowed like sand through his fingers. And then, Luqman wanted to keep up appearances. Finally, Marina's name reminded him of an old woman in his village who used to chase him as a boy with a bucket of water every time he came near her mangy cat. All this led him to give in and accept the waiter's "...all ze nite."

When Luqman stretched out over Marina, it was like sinking into a bed of lush grass, with the sun of his blood-swollen veins falling upon her sweet, glistening waters.

And when the slumber crept to his eyes, it was uncommonly peaceful. As he fell asleep, head gently nodding, he murmured, "Look here, comrades. See how I've taken a Communista!"

That's what they used to call Russia in his village, the

Communista. And that's what Luqman started calling Marina, the gleaming white Russian girl.

--

Drenched in his own sweat, limbs splayed, Luqman got up reluctantly. He had to get up or the festival would pass him by. He didn't want to miss a single detail, no matter how small. He would be in the front row so that nothing would block his view.

He put the coffee pot on the burner. Then he lit a cigarette, one of the few he had come across the previous night, and went off to the toilet. He lifted the seat cover, dropped his boxers, and sat down. What is it that turned the white of the sink and the bathtub to this disgusting gray, given that the water hadn't worked for years?

"Peace returned, but the water never came back," Luqman said to himself while carefully calculating what his bowels were pushing out, the amount of water he would need to flush it down, and how much was left in his plastic containers. He would ask the doorman to fill the bathtub with water from the broken water main below the stairs. No, he would do that himself when he came home. Doormen were no longer what they used to be, and neither was Luqman.

He leaned forward a bit, lifting his rear end so he could throw the cigarette butt through the hole in the seat. As soon as he settled back, two eyes, shining with their sharp blackness, came into view.

It was standing in the small window, frozen in place and alert but without embarrassment. It stared at Luqman and didn't twitch a whisker, as though it weren't afraid. As though it were never afraid.

Luqman thought, "If only my AK-47 were within reach, I would raise it slowly, put my eye to the sights, aim right between its eyebrows, and carefully squeeze the trigger. I'd nail it!"

He would nail it, and he would enjoy watching the bastard's skull explode, its brains burst out, and its blood splatter in all directions. After that, he would go over to grab it and throw it on the ground. He would stand over its carcass, kicking it and stomping on it with both feet until its guts squeezed out of its stomach, mouth, ears.

If only... But Luqman's AK-47 wasn't within reach, and the bastard's eyes kept watching him with their sharp blackness. What was it looking at? What gave it such a feeling of superiority? His nakedness, of course! Luqman's nakedness, his genitals exposed, boxers bunched up around his feet.

"You strip a person naked," the Albino used to tell him. "You return him to his roots, to the caves. Then you put him in the bathroom and do what you want to him."

The Albino wasn't an albino; he wasn't even blond. He was short and had the face of a boy who would never reach puberty. He was like those kids who came too late, whose parents insisted on bringing them into the world long after the natural time for childbearing. Maybe that was why Luqman had loved him. Maybe that was why

Luqman had adopted him.

"I am the Lord's right hand," the Albino used to say, "and the wrath of the Lord is great."

Luqman used to ask him, "But why the water, Albino? Why do you force them to take a shower first?" The Albino would answer with a laugh, "I baptize them so they might be purified of their sins. So they meet their Lord repenting and seeking forgiveness!"

It is the Lord who gives and the Lord who takes away, and it was He who summoned the Albino one evening.

The Albino died. But not in a shelling. He wasn't assassinated. No mobile roadblock snatched him away, nor did his enemies ambush him. Fate caught him at home one night, after his mother, Lurice, had prepared him supper.

He had gone back to visit her after a long time away. He brought her an assortment of bags and gifts because he was her only child and used to take care of her. Lurice wasn't aware of the nature of the Albino's activities. He told her he helped the poor and the needy, distributing food and supplies to them. She believed him, and she prayed for his safety, staying up all night and addressing the picture of the Blessed Virgin.

"My mother is a saint, Luqman. If she found out, she would die on the spot."

But it was the Albino who had died.

Lurice told us, his friends, "He expired in his bed at night. A heart attack, most likely." She didn't weep. She spoke like a doctor giving a diagnosis to strangers. Her head was uncovered, and her hair was completely white, as though it had changed colors in a matter of days. And she didn't weep.

We, too, his friends, who hadn't learned the news of his death until days later when we started missing him and came to his mother for news, we did not cry for him.

Maybe we understood something more about him from that visit. We remembered that "the Albino" had only been a nickname, and that he actually bore the name of the saint whose picture we saw displayed prominently in the parlor.

The saint looked more like a fierce warrior than he did a saint. A naked sword was in one hand, and in the other he held, by its hair, the head of a man who lay prostrate at his feet. In his anger, the glowering saint stood ramrod straight like a tornado in the center of a field sown with fire, destruction, and the bodies of the slain: a picture of Saint Elias, the patron saint of our comrade— the Albino—who had died.

--

By the time Luqman finished emptying his bowels, the bastard had disappeared from the bathroom window. Had it gone back to where it came from, or had it used Luqman's momentary state of distraction to jump inside and crouch in some corner?

Luqman returned to the main room and cast a quick glance around the place. It would be impossible to find it amid such a mess.

He went off to the kitchen and began looking around while spooning coffee and sugar into the water of the coffeepot. There were piles of dirty dishes, food scraps, cigarette butts, and spots of congealed fat. If the bastard took up residence here, it would think it had arrived at a five-star hotel.

No, he ought to visit Salaam as soon as possible. The house could endure no further neglect. He would stop by her place of work, invent excuses for her about some illness, his search for a job, or his embarrassment at being broke and unable to take her out for lunch or dinner.

Luqman extinguished his cigarette in the dregs of his coffee cup. Then he resumed lathering his chin so it wouldn't dry out. He hung the small mirror on the window latch after opening one of the panes, and he began to shave.

The light here wasn't any better than in the bathroom. They had shut off his electricity because he hadn't paid his bills for the past six months. How could he pay after the peace came, when electricity began costing an arm and a leg? Oh, well. Fifteen years of the country being plunged into darkness, and then they turned off his electricity. He'd show them he had the eyes of a mole. That he was used to seeing in the pitch-black even better than he could see in broad daylight.

As the razor pressed its edge against Luqman's neck, it traced a fine, dark thread that soon leaked blood. Luqman looked around, but he didn't find anything to help him. He went over to the bed and used an edge of the embroidered sheet, the colors of which would ably perform the task of camouflaging the blood. It occurred to him to light a cigarette, but he remembered that his own pack had been empty for a while. He poured some aftershave in the hollow of his palm, which he splashed onto his face, opening up his lungs. It had been a gift from Marina and was always refreshing, just like her impossibly tall, snowy whiteness.

He lifted the dark suit he kept for such occasions from its hook and spread it gently on the bed. This, too, had been a gift. From Salaam. Its stark color, like a school uniform, resembled her. It was navy, and the shirt was white, according to her taste. This is how Salaam dreamed of seeing him at a wedding. Their wedding.

--

Luqman descended the stairs with a smooth chin and a spring in his step. If it weren't too embarrassing, he would have whistled a tune.

When he reached the entryway, an odor of uncertain origin filled his nostrils. He stopped and looked over at the doorman's apartment. What if he went over and started kicking the door violently, shouting, "Open up, bitch! Open up, or I'll blow you away!"

Luqman smiled a bit sadly. That time had come and gone. There was a time when the earth itself trembled at his footsteps. But the balance of power was no longer in his favor. Now the doorman with the weird accent was backed up by someone stronger than Luqman and Luqman's clan. The building's residents all feared this man who never carried out the duties that fell on a doorman's shoulders. On top of that, the noisy commotion of his kids filled the whole building, day and night.

Luqman opened the front door, and a big rat jumped in front of him. He nearly fell over backwards. He shouted at it, "In the bathroom window and in the doorway, eh, bastard?! Inside the building and outside too!"

Luqman quickly went out before his cries woke the doorman—who never granted him so much as a "good morning"—and gave him an excuse to verbally abuse Luqman in that weird accent of his.

CHAPTER 3

The light hadn't gotten out of bed again that morning. The were still many clouds, wandering back and forth indecisively. They didn't move on, nor were they persuaded yet of the need to dump their load of rain.

Luqman went down the street, thinking, "Perfect weather for a storm. Yellow clouds and no wind. Certainly time for a storm. Or maybe an earthquake."

The shutters of the shops were closed. Where could he get a pack of smokes now? When he got to the festival, if he hadn't found an open shop, maybe he would ask someone to give him a cigarette.

Here was that vile half-human coming, as always, between the cars! Coming, indeed, on his hands. Half of a human, relieved of his lower body, moving with the speed of a hare—or a tortoise. Whenever Luqman went out, he saw him. And whenever Luqman saw him, he was seized with an overwhelming desire to kick him. Didn't he ever sleep?

If Luqman still owned his Range Rover, he would have slowed down a little to give the beggar the idea that Luqman would offer him a bit of money. That way, the beggar would stop and wait. Suddenly, at the last minute, Luqman would turn the wheel and run the beggar down. He would enjoy the screech of his rubber tires crushing bone. If only...

The mendicant half-human raised his hand with a pack of cigarettes. Luqman reached down to pay and take it. The beggar smiled! Oh, well. Luqman would put off the kick until the next time. Today he would forgive him on account of the smokes and his own good mood, and especially because of the festival.

But one morning, Luqman would get up just for him. This dead man who was up for sale. Or rather, this dead man who was free for the taking. Let's say half a dead man. And when there was no one who would demand blood money, isn't half a dead man better than a whole?

--

He arrived to find they had beaten him there.

A surging human sea of mixed ages, inclinations, religions, colors, and associations. They gathered together in every open space. The edges of the crowd hung like bunches of grapes from balconies, rooftops, electrical poles, and delivery trucks.

Goddamn them! When did they wake up? Most likely they had spent the night here to arrive before him, he and all the other sleepers.

Luqman forced his way with difficulty between shoulder-to-shoulder lines of humanity, heading for the edge of the square where someone had put up a tent with some low chairs underneath.

Out of breath, Luqman said, "A cup of coffee, please."

The vendor said, "I wish I could! Between yesterday morning and dawn today, I've sold more than I normally sell in a week. I don't have any coffee left. What would you say to a cup of tea?"

Luqman nodded in assent.

The vendor went on, "Man, everyone has been bored to death! We kill ourselves for festivals!"

Luqman looked over to where the people were gathering. "No kidding, and what a festival it is!" he responded. Meanwhile, his eyes roamed over the tables, covered with breakfast, that formed a circle around the square with the platform in its center. The platform was roped off to prevent the onlookers from getting too close.

The occasion was marked by a festive commotion.

Coffee, juice, and snack vendors made their way among the people, who had come alone and in groups. Vendors clinked glasses and tapped colored bottles with metal bottle openers, urging everyone to have fun and celebrate.

There were cookies, grilled corn, boiled fava beans, sandwiches, sweets.

Mothers spread blankets on the ground and took out their breasts to suckle their babies in plain sight.

Old folks were carried from their homes and set on low folding chairs.

Soldiers and police officers gathered here and there. They spoke in low voices as they smoked and watched the crowd out of the corners of their eyes.

There were photographers, reporters, tape recorders, cameras, telephoto lenses.

There were Boy Scout troops, civil defense squads, and other groups. Placards on sticks bore illustrations and slogans supporting one thing or another.

A pack of teenagers carried a drum and a small tambourine, improvising the cheering section that would have been seen at a soccer game or a wedding.

Girls wore their Sunday dresses and adorned themselves with their prettiest bracelets and necklaces. Perhaps they would turn some heads or catch the long-awaited husband.

And the men! Such manly men! Fathers and sons. They played backgammon, twirled their mustaches, or scratched their heads with a satisfied air, all the while guarding their women from stray glances and wayward thoughts.

"How did they know?" Luqman asked the vendor while dissolving an extra spoonful of sugar in his plastic cup.

"How did they know?" the vendor repeated. "From every television and radio! They've been announcing the news, day and night for a week."

Luqman said, "Sure, but they didn't specify the date, only the place."

The vendor said, "That's the way they are. They always think they are smarter than the people. All the same, the news leaked out. Don't ask me how, but it leaked. Of course, if they had announced the date, you would have seen the entire country on the march, and—"

The vendor had not finished his sentence when he noticed movement in the front rows surrounding the platform. He dropped whatever he was holding and ran. Luqman followed.

A convoy arrived, composed of a truck, together with some cars and motorcycles, their sirens blaring. They stopped. A number of police officers got out and formed a solid perimeter between the public and the area near the platform on all sides. As Luqman watched them, a smile came over his face. "They think they're in a movie, and—God!—they are acting it up!"

The crowd applauded. The teenagers' drum resounded with vigorous pounding. The graceful torsos of girls who were born to dance swayed back and forth.

The vendor grumbled, "Man, come on! We're tired! What are they waiting for?"

Luqman shrugged his shoulders. He turned away, having decided to move out of the vicinity so the vendor wouldn't spoil the spectacle for him with his chattering questions and stupid comments.

"God! It's an awesome sight!" he heard one person say as he forced his way with effort through the compact throng.

A woman shouted, still chewing her food, "Where

are these heroes? Let's go! Bring them out so we can see them!"

If it were up to Luqman, he would have rained down blows upon her and kicked her fat belly. He would have yanked her hair back and spat in her dirty mouth, full of food. If only...Ah, rest in peace, Albino! Everything you said about them is true. Scum! I swear to God, they are even worse than scum. A herd. Animals deserving slaughter at the guillotine!

Luqman stopped in despair. An immense desire to go back home to bed would have overpowered him had he not noticed that elegant, pretty blond standing nearby, apart from all the rest. She carried a radio transmitter in one hand, and she was fixing her hair with the other.

A huge man mounted the platform and said in the loudest imaginable voice, "If it isn't completely silent this very instant, I'm going to clear the place out!"

Complete and total silence reigned.

The rear door of the truck opened. The two "heroes" got out and stood holding onto each other. The crowd went wild. Women trilled, children whistled. The two men lowered their eyes in shame. No, not shame. Something like a daze. Just like what happens to amateur performers when they go up on stage for the first time and are surprised by the size of the audience.

Luqman looked at the broadcaster. He saw her lifting the transmitter to her mouth and pouring into it a veritable flood of words mixed with saliva. What could she be saying?

He turned back to the "heroes" of the festival. They were clinging to each other even more than before. Oh, well. He'd leave them for a while and then return. Strictly speaking, these were only the preliminary preparations. The decisive moment, the essential moment he ought not to miss, was when they mounted the platform. Everything else was just details.

Luqman drew away from the throng in order to approach the broadcaster and come into her line of sight. She turned towards him. He smiled at her, and she smiled back flirtatiously. Then she returned to her transmitter, spitting out her stream of words.

A radio broadcaster! Luqman felt a stab of disappointment, and he pursed his lips. He would have preferred the smile to come from a television broadcaster.

He stood with his arms folded, leaning against a tree, his back turned to the stage where the festivities were unfolding. He began to stare at the broadcaster, not taking his eyes off her. He observed her closely this time, he did more than observe her. His ravenous gaze took her captive and began to grope her firm, luscious body. He knew she felt it from the beads of sweat gathering on her upper lip, which quivered slightly, and from the tone of her voice, which shook and jumped all over the place.

"...and after pronouncing the death sentence passed against them by the criminal court, the sole civilian judge approached the condemned and asked them whether they had any last wishes, or anything they wanted to say, before the sentence was carried out. The first man was shaking.

Tears ran from his eyes, and his face had gone white. He said, 'My last wish is that my mother won't fall dead from sorrow on account of me.' The other said, 'I don't have any last wishes.' His strength failed him, and he wept."

Luqman put his hand to his crotch. Come on! Get up, Partner! Stand up and enjoy the view of this splendid blond festival.

The broadcaster lifted a hand to scratch her breast with long, shiny red fingernails until a hard nipple protruded distinctly through her thin, white shirt. She produced the same effect on Luqman, only double.

The bitch! Luqman thought to himself. She was aroused but not at all distracted. Indeed, she went on smoothly without losing her train of thought.

"...They became even more terrified when they saw the scaffold and the nooses. They were unable to walk and visibly wilted after four steps. The first collapsed entirely and fell to the ground; the other stumbled. This prevented them from being dressed in the customary white execution gowns. So the guards carried them onto the platform."

Luqman looked around. No one was watching him... watching them. Everyone was fixed upon the platform and what was taking place there. What if his partner gave the broadcaster a "good morning"? After being constricted, it could get some relief and a breath of fresh air...

"...The executioner swiftly put the head of the first man through the noose. Then he moved to the other and wrapped his neck with the rope. The wooden platform beneath their feet fell away, and the two men dangled in the air and began to jerk around until, after a few moments, they gave up the ghost. When the sentence was carried out, all the people cheered jubilantly and applauded. The number of those witnessing the execution is estimated to be in the thousands, from all different regions. The packed balconies and rooftops of the buildings surrounding the square testify to the size of the assembly."

--

Luqman lifted his head and said, "Why don't we go to your place?"

"Because I live with my parents," she answered, grabbing his ears and bringing his mouth back down to her crotch.

Luqman lifted his head again and said, "No problem. What do you say we go to my place then?"

The broadcaster, both irritable and mean-spirited, responded, "My shift isn't over yet! But in any case, it's fine. You can leave right now, if you want to."

Luqman laughed. "Are you serious? Where would I go? There's no need to get angry, Miss...I'm at the lady's command!"

The young lady dug her fingernails into Luqman's back when she came, then her face relaxed all at once. She pushed herself back up in her seat and opened her eyes to stare at Luqman.

When Luqman moved to get on top of her, she pushed him away. "Sorry, I can't help you. I'm still a virgin."

Luqman smiled and nodded. He pulled away a hair that was stuck to his tongue and said, "No problem!"

But when he asked her to repay him in kind, she shook back her hair and fanned a hand in front of her face to show how uncomfortable she was from the heat. Luqman repeated his question in another way, grabbing her hand to...She jerked it away and fumbled with her key as she put it in the ignition and started the car. She folded her arms and began staring straight in front of her at the road. She was shaking.

Luqman kept watching her silently. Then he said, "Can I see you again?"

She turned and slapped his cheek. "Hell, no! Forget you ever saw me today. The best thing for you to do is forget about it. If you don't, I'll send someone who'll make you forget your own name, got it?" She leaned across him to open the door. Then she pushed him out with her bare foot.

Luqman stood with his hands in his pockets. He lifted his eyes to the sky, laden with clouds. "That's life, Partner! You win some, you lose some."

He walked off.

CHAPTER 4

The neighborhood was still asleep.

Luqman would have thought he was in a rich neighborhood, were it not for the plastic bags, their bellies torn open and spilling out their garbage entrails. Masked ghosts, showing nothing but their eyes, sifted through the piles.

This was a new species, thought Luqman. The "unseen families," as they had come to be called. It was the species of those who only went out under the cover of night, when they were turned out from the places to which they repaired during the daylight hours. First the war, and later the peace, had stripped them of their teeth, their fingernails, and their ability to buy. This species was distinct from the species of beggars in that its members maintained some dignity and pride, some fear and shame, such that they were not willing to be seen in used clothing, even if that meant they would consume half-eaten food.

Luqman saw these unseen ones scattered around the edges of the neighborhood like deformed insects or shattered trees with charred fruit. He turned his eyes away so as not to disturb the pleasure he felt upon entering the intimacy of this humble neighborhood, which resembled a blue bedroom sunk in a deep slumber.

Whenever Luqman entered the neighborhood, he felt he was going down instead of up, even though it stood atop a small hill.

Maybe it was the flowerpots that decorated the door-ways abutting the small street. The entrances only went up two or three steps, as though to stay close and extend an invitation, welcoming the passerby to have a seat and make himself comfortable for a few moments. Or a few hours.

Or maybe it was the low buildings, not more than two or three stories tall, with their wan and faded colors and their windows, protected by airy, delicate curtains decorated with borders of lace.

"Thank God," Luqman murmured to himself. There were still neighborhoods that preserved their modesty in this debauched city, crowded as it was with buildings that looked like mythical animals reminiscent of a bygone era or one still to come. Fanciful buildings, built for fanciful princes, shooting up every day, everywhere, insolent and disdainful. The buildings had strange, seductive names, enticing designs, and specifications that beggared the imagination. They rose up and remained half finished, hanging in the air. Like ghosts. Like freaks of nature, growing taller and more absurd. Like powerful men when they go mad and suffer delusions of grandeur, afflicted by hallucinations, amnesia, and nervous breakdowns.

Perhaps it was for all those reasons that Luqman loved Salaam's neighborhood and felt a sense of ease and security there.

--

Salaam was a few years older than him and had never been beautiful. Maybe that was why the Albino, who hated women and didn't feel safe around them, loved her.

She had been his neighbor and used to bring trays of coffee, juice, sandwiches, and other food down to "the gang," when, at the beginning of the war, they took it upon themselves to stay up late, guarding the residential neighborhoods from expected raids. That was after the people of the city had been divided into thieves and heroes, good and evil.

The Albino never touched her. Whenever Luqman would tease him by alluding to her big butt, which jiggled at every step, he would say, "She has more honor than all other women combined!" And when Luqman would respond, "What makes you so sure?" the Albino would become furious, sputtering and struggling to speak, his face turning red. Luqman would fall silent and apologize. He was never afraid for himself during the Albino's bouts of rage, though he did fear for the Albino.

Salaam was Luqman's inheritance from the Albino.

If only the Albino's taste had been a little better! Why did you choose precisely her, Albino? What drew you to her? "A fine metal thread, too hard and solid for your bombs to destroy, Luqman," he used to answer.

And when a shell mowed down Salaam's parents, hiding from a bombardment in the shelter, the Albino exulted joyously. Luqman had never seen him so worked up.

"She didn't cry, Luqman!" the Albino was saying. "And when I went to comfort her, she looked at me for a long time and said with a touch of reproach, 'You offer me your condolances for two old people, Albino, while the gang are dying by the dozens, no, the hundreds?'"

On that day, the Albino was certain that he loved her, that he had loved her for a long time, from the very first instant. He kissed her on the hand and the head and fired off twenty rounds in her honor.

--

Luqman knocked on the door. This was another point in Salaam's favor: a wooden door with opaque glass; no doorbell or buzzer.

She woke up.

He heard the bedroom door creak. He heard her heavy feet in their slippers shuffling over the old, yellow floor tiles. If only she would lose a little weight, then may- be...Even if she lost weight, what would he do about her age? She was over forty. What about her hairy chin? What about her face? Whenever he saw it, he felt that the skin was sagging and melting away. What would he do with her cracked lips? And what about her small, dry breasts? Her ass! Of course, if he focused on her ass, then maybe...The thought had crossed his mind. But if he set aside the rest of the details and kept the ass like it was, wouldn't it, too, appear with surprises of its own?

The door opened.

He hadn't been wrong. He had surprised her by coming this morning. And she surprised him with her puffy eyes and the way her short hair stood up on the side of her head like a cat that had been electrocuted.

She smiled and embraced him. The odor of her breath shocked him, and her oily sweat stuck to his cheek. He pushed her away. "Someone might see us," he said.

She looked at him kindly and showed him in.

"Be careful not to step on the traps! The rats are killing me," she said. She disappeared into the bathroom.

Luqman heard the splashing of the shower as he took a turn around the sitting room. Old furniture, without a speck of dust. He touched things. Cold and clean. He pushed open the bedroom door and saw the bed. White sheets, clean and white like snow. Like the amazing body of Marina. No! He should put Marina out of his mind for now. Out of respect for Salaam, for all she did on his behalf without any payment, or for the sake of some recompense that he kept putting off.

At the beginning, when he began visiting her after the Albino's death, she had maintained a definite reticence.

Then, towards the end of the war, when the comrades began to be hunted down and thrown in prison, she came to him one evening and said, "Don't stay here a single moment longer! You'll be safe at my place." She had gathered his things for him and brought him to her house, saying, "Stay here. No one will see you or turn you in."

No one saw him again for weeks.

She would come home to him from her work at the telephone exchange—"the Central," as it was called—bringing news about strangers and relatives, about allies and enemies. She would make dinner in the evening and talk to him about the Albino and about her life, which had been shattered by the Albino's death. She would talk about her terrible luck, which had robbed her of a friend, a brother, a husband, and a father for the children she would never have. She would fall silent for a while and then conclude her speech by swearing she would never again think about men.

A few more weeks.

Here was Salaam, enjoying his presence and no longer talking about the Albino when she made dinner. Deep down, she had begun to cherish the dream of marrying Luqman. He figured that out from the news of raids and detentions, which she started inventing sometimes, exaggerating the details in order to make him afraid and keep him there. Later, he had no doubt about it when she began to shower him with gifts and embarrass him with effusive gestures of respect.

Another few weeks.

Here was Luqman, enjoying in turn his free stay at this luxurious hotel. But Salaam surprised him. She didn't limit herself to that kind of persuasion alone. She began resorting to an endless litany of laudatory ethical descriptions, which she began hanging on her breast as badges, or jabbing into his chest like safety pins.

"Isn't a true woman the housewife rather than the fashion model? Aren't honor and morals the two essential pillars for the success of the institution of marriage? Doesn't one hand need its sister in order to clap?"

And so on, with other enigmatic and loaded sentences that aimed at leading him into a marriage trap.

At first, Luqman let himself get caught up in Salaam's game because he believed he was the one calling the shots. He would respond to her questions by advocating the counterarguments to her face, feeding that game of incursions and increasing her zealous efforts to persuade him. But as she became more aggressive and no longer stopped at the border, he realized his danger and the need to escape with his skin intact before losing his chance.

When he let her know he intended to leave, she became furious and slapped him. Then she used her fear for him as a pretext for his staying, claiming his stubbornness was an act of suicide. But by now, she had regained her senses and become calm after a long torment. Perhaps she had despaired. Or else she understood and was content with his occasional visits.

She still pampered him. She loved him in silence and pampered him. Nevertheless, despite all that she did for him, Luqman didn't fall into the trap. Instead, he would "remain faithful," as he put it, to the memory of a friend he used to have. He wouldn't touch her in order to make her understand that he, for his part, saw in her a woman he respected, even venerated. She was the wife he didn't deserve, he who had no past or future.

He persuaded her of all this without needing to use words. Just looks and sighs that Salaam took days, even weeks, to interpret. Until the time came for a subsequent visit and a new puzzle, a riddle wrapped inside an enigma, which he would drop in her lap to distract her from him. She would devote herself to taking apart the riddle, and he would slip away for periods of varying length—according to the amount of provisions he obtained from her—never more than a month...

--

Salaam came out of the bathroom followed by a cloud of soap and perfume. She was looking much better now. Well, a little better anyway.

Luqman went with her into the kitchen. She made breakfast. Cream, yogurt, za'atar, fried eggs, and cheeses. Fresh mint leaves, tomatoes, and cucumbers. Warm bread, as though fresh from the bakery oven.

He sat across the table from her. As she was cutting the food and seasoning it with salt and spices, she said a little flirtatiously, "What got you up so early like this? Or after being out all night as usual, did you get fed up and remember Salaam?"

Luqman smiled. Now the sweat was beading on her temples and her cracked lips. After a bit, the spots would appear under her bushy armpits. A sweaty woman. That was more than he could endure. Salaam was a woman for the winter. Marina was a cool breeze for the summer.

"I didn't sleep yesterday," Salaam went on.

"Why not?"

"After midnight and after two sleeping pills, the Albino's mother woke me up. She had come down with some kind of fever or delirium. She began stomping on the floor of the room right above my head, calling, 'Salaam! Come quickly, Salaam!' I got up like a mad-women and raced up the stairs four at a time. I thought someone had broken in, to rob or kill her. But I found her all alone in her nightgown. I gave her a sedative and told her, 'Calm down, Lurice!' Which she did. I waited un-til I was sure she was okay, and she fell asleep near dawn. That's when I came down to sleep...Why are you lighting a cigarette? You haven't eaten anything yet!"

Luqman took a deep drag on the cigarette, leaned his chair back, and puffed out smoke rings. He ought to lead her away from this chattering she loved and was so good at, to induce her gradually to ask about his affairs. He'd plant a bomb for her, and he'd nail it. He intended to see Marina that evening. But seeing Marina required cash, and Salaam had the cash.

Salaam made coffee, still running at the mouth: "Poor Lurice! She said she saw the Albino in her dream. He was staring at her wide-eyed, and when she asked him what was the matter, he didn't answer. He didn't utter a sound. In the end, he came over to her and started smoothing her hair and caressing her face until both his hands were around her neck, and he began squeezing so hard she felt she was choking."

Salaam's dress was sticking to her butt. The hem, which had been tied up, went up further to reveal little purplish-blue veins in the crease of her knees. She stood in front of the sink, cleaning off the plates and rinsing them. The lines of her underwear were visible. They pressed into her butt cheeks in the attempt to hold them in, giving the appearance of four distinct sections. Salaam actually had two butts: one inside her underwear and one outside.

Salaam was cleaning the dishes, and her butt was talking vigorously. Luqman was sweating. His partner stood straight up to reply to Salaam's butt.

What's wrong with you that you get excited and stand up without permission? Take a good look, Partner, and make no mistake: what you see in this kitchen is only Salaam!

So what? Put one of the thick plastic bags over her head to hide her face. Then you can imagine she is some other woman.

Is that how you express your deep gratitude? Fine, and then what, Partner?

Shove her against the sink, lift up her skirt, tear her panties in half, and—

Take it easy, Partner! If you did her just once, Salaam would never again leave you in peace. She'd suck your blood until you dried out and withered, and all life left you for good. Or would that make you happy? Is that what you want?

I know it's all too much and you're fed up, but doesn't patience have its limits? I've been in torment since dawn, and whose fault is it but yours?

And how is it my fault, Partner, that the blond broadcaster was a vile slut and a lowlife whore? Come on! Forget Salaam and her butt. Even if I gave you what you wanted, you'd be disappointed. Listen, if you stay worked up—

"Luqman, I won't be long. I'll take Lurice a tray of food. Then I'll come right back," Salaam said as she went out.

Luqman grabbed his partner, and the two of them went into the bathroom.

CHAPTER 5

She flashed her wide smile as she threw him the car keys. He hated her. How he hated her! If only he hadn't gone to her this morning. She knew exactly why he had come, and she was leading him on. She kept making him wait in order to test how long he could endure.

An ugly spinster, but cunning. That's how Luqman saw her now. He wanted to accelerate as fast as possible, open the door, and jump out. The car would follow its course through the trees and crash into the stone wall. It would bounce into the air, and Salaam's body, trapped inside the iron frame, would be pulverized on the jagged rocks and dried grass below. If only...

Salaam jammed a cassette into the jaws of the tape deck and pressed play. A woman started singing, lethargically at first, but then she set in with vigor.

Luqman had closed the window against the thick traffic and dust, but he opened it now. A wind blew over him.

The air had become slightly cooler after filtering through the stone pines that passed by on the shoulders of the winding road going up the mountain.

If it weren't for these dense clouds, Luqman's mood would have shifted entirely. He would even have felt something that resembled joy. Not bad. His mood had lifted a little. Now he was looking over at Salaam, and the wink he sent her didn't betray the animosity he had felt just moments before.

He demanded a lot of her, and he got mad at her when she acted like a woman. It's okay, Luqman, if she's stubborn sometimes. No matter what she is, Salaam will always be a woman, and she'll have a woman's moods. Let her indulge herself from time to time. What if she were a dog? Wouldn't it be her right to ask you for a bit of attention and tenderness? It's good you were willing to go with her. An orphaned woman with no one looking after her. It's a fine thing you're doing, something she'll repay with a handful of dollars, hopefully. Hope for the best, and it'll come your way. Smile, and the world smiles with you. So does Salaam.

Luqman breathed deeply. He hummed along to the song coming from the tape player. Then he looked at Salaam and said, joking and flirtatious, "Salaam, oh, Salaam!"

--

With obvious irritation, the director said, "Only doctors

can bring their cars into the sanatorium." She turned to Salaam and continued, "If your fiancé doesn't park the car outside, you won't see Saleem, and I'll cancel your weekly visits!"

They didn't respond.

Salaam didn't respond out of fear for Saleem, her younger brother. Every Sunday, she came to visit him in this free, government-run institution. She brought different kinds of sweets and food. She gave him clean clothes and brought home with her the clothes that had gotten dirty. If only she had been in a position to put him in a private clinic, or to take him to be treated in a foreign country equipped with better techniques! If only...

As for Luqman, he was afraid that Salaam, if the director prevented her from visiting, would take her brother out of the state asylum. It had taken him long weeks of suffering to persuade her of the need to commit him. Taking Saleem out would mean bringing him back to the house, which would require hiring a private nurse to keep him safe and care for his needs. More particularly, that would mean an additional expense and money set aside out of reach, just to benefit that idiot, Saleem.

Salaam leaned over the trunk of the car and took out some bags. She headed towards the entrance, saying, "Why don't you come with me? He'd be happy to see you."

Luqman replied that he had no desire to run into that slut of a director again, otherwise he'd end up doing something he'd regret. He went on to say he'd wait for her in the garden. Salaam agreed and said she wouldn't be long.

Luqman's mood became sullen again after he saw her head up the stairs and go inside. God alone knew what Miss Salaam—Spinster Salaam—would force him to do. Why didn't she give him what he wanted and let him go his own way? Why did she insist on torturing him like this? Goddamn her and her handful of dollars that she doled out to him with an eyedropper! A miserly spinster who forced him to come to the insane asylum! What did she need the money for? She didn't pay rent since she had inherited her apartment from family. Did she have any expenses other than food, drink, and some clothes? Fine, what about the rest of her salary? Why didn't she give it to Luqman? In order to spite him. She wanted to bust his balls every time he came to her. So she could suck his blood, wreck his way of life, ruin his good moods.

The whore! All women were whores, no exceptions. Even his mother had been a whore. She would beat him for the most trivial reasons, even for no reason at all. She would beat him until blood ran from his mouth. And when his father came home, she would go complain about him. Then his father would beat him too and tie him to the tree for hours.

Why all the beating, Luqman? Because you killed a mangy cat, or you threw a rock through a window, or you hung a rabbit. Your parents cherished animals above you, and they would beat you rather than blame the neighbors and villagers who brought complaints.

When you left them a little before the war broke
out, you went away unapologetic, not looking back and
fervently hoping to be gone forever. The only permissible
motive for going back would be revenge.

And during the war, when your star was rising, they
didn't leave you alone. Instead, they started coming to you,
time after time, to seek your help: Your brothers are naked...
the earth is parched...the rains haven't come...your mother
is sick...your father needs treatment...the dirt roof of the
house is about to collapse, and so on without end. Pay for it,
Luqman! Give, Luqman! Be a sport, Luqman! Show compassion, have mercy, feel pity...and pay for it, Luqman, pay!

And when the war ended, when your own good
fortune was reversed and your pockets became empty
again, they turned away and forgot you. When you asked
them for help, they started whining and griping again:
Where would we get anything? What you gave us wasn't
enough to finish the four-story building. We were forced
to mortgage the land and take out loans...Why do you
yell like this? Deep down, you've always been good for
nothing, and you can't teach an old dog new tricks. Leave,
and don't come back! We, your family, want nothing to do
with you. We do not acknowledge you. And we'll call the
police on you if you don't stop yelling...

--

"If you don't stop yelling, I'll put you in the straitjacket
and lock you up!"

Salaam ran and put her hand over Saleem's mouth. She promised the attendant that he would stop yelling after a little, and that he, the attendant, would be rewarded if he let her have a few extra minutes with her little brother.

"Little?" responded the attendant. "People have grandchildren at his age. What's more, he riles the others up, and if they get riled up and start shouting too, what am I supposed to do? What would I say to the director? Visits usually take place through the bars. I've already brought you in to him, and that's against the rules. What else do you want from me, Miss Salaam? For me to lose my job? Shame on you! I have kids!"

Salaam smiled and said, "Don't you see? He has calmed down. He yelled so that I wouldn't leave, so that I'd stay with him longer. Didn't I promise you a gift? Let me stay, and you'll be rewarded."

"Fine," answered the attendant. "Bring me the gift. I'll be back in a quarter-hour."

Saleem sat back down near his sister, Salaam. He started knocking his head against her shoulder again, imploring. She looked around and saw that the others were all calm. They, too, looked at her, imploring.

Salaam opened the buttons of her shirt and thought about the great sacrifices she made for her brother, to keep him looking human. What about the others? Didn't they have parents and siblings? She saw their torn clothing, their long, dirty fingernails, their bare, blackened feet, and their faces filled with cuts, bruises, and inflamed pimples leaking pus. Then she resumed gazing at Saleem's face and thanked God.

He threw his head against her chest, imploring. She slipped her hand in to her breast, brought it out, and gave it to him. Saleem sucked with his eyes closed while the others watched. Sometimes she thought he tricked her with his yelling fits so that she would give him her breast. How did this memory come back to him? How did he remember that she had suckled him when he had been only a few years old?

She was the one who had raised him. Their mother had given birth to him when she was almost fifty. Salaam had grown up as an only child after her mother's womb had decided not to bear any more children. Then it changed its mind suddenly and brought forth Saleem. How wonderful her little brother had been! Thanks to Salaam. For Salaam is the one who raised him. She stayed up at night with him, fed him, rocked him, put him to bed, taught him...and suckled him. Until...

Until the war came.

The war was responsible for her losing him, for his losing his mind, for his mind losing its sense. Or else it was the Albino, whom Saleem began accompanying during his nightly rounds and his nighttime work.

All she remembered was that Saleem came home one day drenched in tears. He said he hated the Albino, that he never wanted to see him again. Salaam slapped him. She slapped him as hard as she could and screamed at him, "Shut up, you coward! You aren't a man.

You're a chicken! I denounce you and your shame, you chickenshit!"

Until she cut off Saleem completely.

She no longer spoke to him. She began going down to "the gang" every night with trays of coffee, juice, snacks, and sandwiches just to spite him. Maybe he would be cured of his cowardice. Maybe he would get it together and return to the righteous struggle.

Until the Albino loved her.

He loved her and saved her from the shame and the schadenfreude of her relatives and neighbors. He protected her just as he protected the people of the neighborhood from death at the hands of their enemies.

Until the Albino proposed to her.

Salaam found her place, and what a place it was! She had a say in things, and the women of the neighborhood started trying to please her. Wasn't she the fiancée of the Albino, this leader of men, at whose passing the surrounding neighborhoods trembled, as well as the neighborhoods beyond?

Until the shell struck the shelter and mowed down their parents, together with Saleem's sound mind.

Her brother began to keep to his room, leaving it rarely. He suffered long periods of insomnia. And if he slept, the nightmares would wake him up. Or his temperature would rise, afflicting him with fever and all kinds of hallucinations.

Until the kid went crazy.

He stood in the door of the house, in view of the

neighbors, and aimed an imaginary machine gun and began firing bullets of spittle. He fired imaginary bullets from an imaginary gun at imaginary people in an imaginary war.

Until the Albino died.

Until the war ended.

Until she went to Luqman to persuade him to hide out in her house.

Until Luqman persuaded her of the necessity of putting Saleem in a mental hospital.

Until she put him in the state sanatorium. She thought Luqman was embarrassed by her brother in front of people, and that if she only got rid of Saleem, Luqman would marry her. He would live with her and compensate her for the long years of deprivation she had known after the Albino's departure.

Until she heard the attendant's steps coming towards her. She pushed Saleem away and tucked her breast inside her shirt, which she buttoned back up. She pulled out a five-dollar bill to give to the attendant, and she hurried away, ignoring her brother's screams and the screeching of his insane cohort.

--

Luqman lit a cigarette. He began wandering through the gardens that surrounded the buildings of the mental institution.

There was nothing better than nature to calm the

nerves. If the war hadn't ended and he were still rich, he would have erected a palace on a high, remote mountain. He would have filled it with rare, exotic animals and lived there alone with snow-white Marina. If only...

Luqman smiled. If anyone heard what was going through his head right now, they would have arrested him immediately and made him a permanent inmate of this asylum. Who would ever believe him if he told of the power, influence, and wealth he used to have? No one! Especially after quick money had become a dream that enticed everyone in this country.

When he saw them walking about with their cell phones, their flashy sunglasses, and their car keys, he wanted to puke. When people were given free rein, everyone became a pompous rooster, crowing and strutting about in public. Up became down, right became left, and decent folk got caught in the grime. The pigs! They were hungry, and they bought cell phones. They were broke, and they took a loan for the entire cost of a car. One nuclear bomb, and it would all be over. A universal conflagration. Each and every one of them annihilated. Then Luqman could rest easy.

One of those bombs you used to be so good at making, Luqman. You would be refreshed, and you would rest easy. Do you remember? God, those were the days! You'd make your bombs, and the buyers would come. Buying and selling. Your business developed and grew, and you became partners with the Albino. You two would secure the supply of bombs and whatever follow-up or servicing they required. Then the Lord made you prosper. And the Lord is generous indeed when he makes someone prosper, Luqman. You had a team of workers that even the Americans envied. You began exporting and working with people of various nationalities until your reputation ranked with the greatest professionals in the world.

And now? And now your fate is tied to half-woman spinsters like Salaam. You, Luqman, who were once able to make the most famous and richest whores in the world get down on their knees. You—

"Luqman? Can it be?"

The speaker didn't give Luqman a chance to recognize his face before he threw himself upon Luqman with an embrace and kisses on both cheeks. The pounding on his back and shoulders continued until Luqman was seized with a fit of coughing. Luqman pushed the man off him and onto the stone bench beside him.

"Najeeb! Is it you? You scared me, man! I thought you were one of the crazies grabbing me. But tell me, why are you dressed like this? What are you doing here? Are you sick too?"

CHAPTER 6

Salaam went into the kitchen to prepare lunch.

When they were riding back from the sanatorium, Luqman hadn't said anything. Salaam asked him whether he was annoyed, but he didn't answer and remained silent. In the end, she became angry too and turned away in disgust.

On the way back, he hadn't stopped thinking about Najeeb. My God! How time flies, and how cruel fate can be when it turns against you.

Luqman had not been sad on anyone's account for a long time. For just as long, Luqman had forgotten the very meaning of sadness. But the pitiful sight of Najeeb made him sadder than he could bear because it reminded him of what had befallen himself.

He got up to pour himself a glass of whiskey. He turned the fan to face him, since the heat had started oppressing his lungs again. Then he sat down once more on the couch and put his feet up on the small coffee table in front of him. He closed his eyes.

What was happening to people? Goddamn "the people"! In the end, what mattered to him were his comrades. What was happening to his comrades? What comrades are you talking about, Luqman? It's been ages since you've seen any of them. You've long forgotten them, and they've forgotten them. Each one scattered to a different place. It's true, you sometimes call a few of them who have left the country. It's not because you miss them or want to reassure yourself about them. Instead, you actually place the call for two reasons: Salaam works in the Central, which means your calls are free, and you hope they might give you some financial help or a plane ticket that would allow you to leave this swamp where you lead a life fit only for a dog.

Najeeb was something else. Why? Because he came from the same place you did. From a war without any connection to his principles and convictions. Because he was like you, making a living on someone else's dime. He seized the opportunity of a lifetime to get rich and become someone, a respected personality, a name that made the earth tremble, someone with authority, admiration, cars, nightclubs, casinos, power, women, and cash.

A savage brute, he hated people and didn't like social interaction. He was a wolf that trusted only himself and his pack. A specialist. A professional. An amazing sniper, just like the Albino was a skilled artist in his torture methods, and you in making bombs—rare types that today have become extinct. You were gods—prophets, rather—deciding fates, believing in your calling, and working alone, high above the level of the common riffraff and the dregs of humanity.

For all these reasons, the sight of Najeeb and his broken dejection made you sad. That's why you listened to him for so long as he told you of his "hellish" plot that would save you both and bring you back to your former splendor and luxury—

"Mother! Luqman!"

Salaam screamed, and Luqman raced to the kitchen after grabbing down from the wall her deceased father's walking stick.

Once again, Luqman saw Salaam's hair standing on end like the fur of an electrocuted cat. But he didn't discover the thief or assailant he expected. Salaam was standing on a chair in the middle of the kitchen, stammering as she spoke and gesticulating wildly.

"The oven!" she said. "Look in the oven!"

Luqman went over and bent down. He saw its eyes staring at him, gleaming with their sharp blackness.

"It's dizzy from the gas," she said. "Hurry, or it will regain consciousness and charge you!"

Luqman smiled. He wouldn't hurry at all. He'd take his good, sweet time, and then a little extra, if that's what it took. Here it was, sitting on the oven's baking rack, perfectly ready. And here was Luqman. He had finally got it, after a long wait and much annoyance.

He turned to Salaam and said, "Go out of the kitchen

and shut the door behind you. Then put something at the bottom to block the crack underneath. Don't open it until I call and say you can come in."

"Let me close the door to the balcony first," she said. Then she went out.

"Welcome, welcome!" whispered Luqman. He bent over, closed the oven door, and turned the gas knob to high. Luqman waited. Then he turned off the gas. You won't die quickly, you bastard! But slowly, leisurely, just as Luqman sees fit.

It occurred to him to ignite the flame on a low setting so that he could roast it peacefully, little by little, until the fur got warm, then the skin, and finally the veins and arteries, which would burst like air bubbles, one after another.

He would roast it. Then he would feed it to Salaam!

Luqman laughed. If he cooked it in her oven, she'd be furious. Maybe even kill him. Miss Hysteria! That was the perfect name for Salaam. Miss Hysteria Clean-Freak herself. This kind of disease was perhaps particularly common among spinsters.

A sound of rustling came from the oven, and of claws scrabbling against metal and glass.

"Have you woken up?" asked Luqman. "Okay. What death do you prefer? Anything in particular? Roasting? How nice that would be! But the matter is complicated because of Salaam. What else is there? Slicing your throat? A stab to the heart? Why shouldn't you have the festival you deserve, seeing as execution by hanging is all the rage these days?"

Of course, he ought to give it a bit more gas, enough to knock it out completely without killing it. How would he gauge it? He'd count to twenty. Or maybe a little more. Until it was good and dizzy, and Luqman could grab it and do with it as he wished.

Luqman turned the knob to full, and a strong odor filled the room. He began to count—"One, two, three"—up to twenty. Then he turned off the gas and waited a moment. He opened the oven.

The rat was on its back with its legs in the air. Grabbing it by its tail, Luqman picked it up and shook it. "Come on! Open your eyes!" It didn't move. He shook it some more, violently. Then he began to smack its body with his hand. "Wake up, you bastard! Get up, you scum! Open your eyes!"

The fucking bastard was dead. It tricked him and died. After dozens of times, it had beaten him once again.

Luqman hurled it across the room. He went over and began jumping on it like a madman until his sandals split it open completely and transformed the corpse into something that held only the vaguest resemblance to the body of a poor rat, killed by gas—saved, that is, from Luqman's vengeance.

--

"I've brought you a surprise, Luqman. Look who's joining us for lunch!"

Lurice was the last thing he needed that day to complete his joy.

"How lovely to see you, Madame Lurice!" Luqman said as he rose to welcome her. "My God, it's been too long! How are you doing? I always ask Salaam about you and your health, and she always reassures me and tells me, 'Madame Lurice is doing better than ever!'"

Lurice didn't respond. She looked around apprehensively, as though she were looking for someone or feared some surprise.

"What's wrong with her?" Luqman asked.

Salaam responded that Lurice saw imaginary people coming to kill her, or to beat and torture her. Salaam told how Lurice's relative, when he visited her one Sunday as usual, made rounds through the entire house to confirm for her that no one was there except them. This reassured Lurice, and she calmed down a bit. That's why Salaam insisted on her coming down for lunch.

"It might do her good to see you and lessen the pain of the Albino's absence. She misses him so much!"

"She still hasn't forgotten him?" Luqman asked.

Salaam answered in disapproval, "Why? Have I forgotten? Have you forgotten? How do you still expect a widow and a mother to forget her only son? What's wrong with you, Luqman?"

"Okay, okay!" Luqman said to calm her down. "I didn't mean anything bad by it. Besides, what's your problem, telling me off in front of her as though I—"

"Don't worry," Salaam said. "She doesn't see you or

hear you. She's always lost, confused, somewhere else mentally. Every now and then she wakes up and comes back to her right mind, and I think she has gotten better because she begins asking me clear questions or wants me to help with some memory or detail that is escaping her."

"Have you taken her to the doctor?" Luqman asked.

"A whole league of doctors," answered Salaam. "Some of them said it was likely the shock that came after the death of a loved one. Others came down on the side of an illness they called schizophrenia. Meanwhile, some maintained it was a nervous breakdown, Alzheimer's, or a neurosis. This went on until Lurice begged me to stop torturing her. She made me swear on the memory of the Albino that I would let her live out the rest of her days at home in peace."

"What about all the expenses, the doctors' examinations, and the costs of the medicine?" Luqman asked anxiously.

Salaam laughed as she shook her head. "Don't worry! I've been spending her own money on her. Don't forget she was one of the most famous seamstresses. She still possesses everything she saved over her entire life, as well as everything the Albino was giving her for years."

"Is it a lot?" Luqman asked, suddenly attentive.

Salaam didn't turn to answer his question. Instead, some confusion rendered her mute. She retreated to the kitchen on the pretext of having to set the table.

Lurice! Are you the prey I've been searching for all this time? The treasure I stumble upon by chance after years of panning for gold? Is it from you, not from her own pockets, that Salaam rains down dollars upon me? Of course! God, how stupid you are, Luqman! Didn't it occur to you? Didn't you ever wonder? How could it escape you that the modest salary from Salaam's job could never support herself, her brother, and you?

Luqman came over to sit down next to Lurice. Lurice was startled and jumped up. She moved away into a corner of the room.

He looked at her contemplatively. If the Albino had lived and grown old, he would have looked like Lurice. Her sunken eyes, her diminutive stature, her skinny pallor—all this reminded Luqman of the Albino.

He took two more steps towards her. She retreated to the door. Why this alarm? Why did she hide her head between her arms as though he were lifting his hand, or a cleaver, to strike her? What was wrong with you, Albino, he wondered. You fell in love with an ugly, miserly spinster, and a cunning one at that. Moreover, you came from a high-strung, feebleminded, simpleton of a mother.

"Have you forgotten me, Mrs. Lurice? I'm Luqman, the Albino's friend, your only son. It's okay. I'll sit down again in my place. You, too, come on back to where you were."

Luqman sat down, and Lurice...she sat down too.

Lurice began smoothing the skirt of her dress against her knees with a continuous, monotonous movement as though she were ironing it, until she suddenly raised her head, looked at Luqman, and finally smiled!

"Luqman! It's so good to see you!"

But her smile quickly disappeared into a look of worried supplication. "Is everything alright? Has anything bad happened to my son?"

"The Albino is perfectly fine, Mrs. Lurice. He asked me to bring you his greetings so that you wouldn't worry. He wanted you to feel at ease about him and to pray for his success."

She remembered him! Finally! It must be one of her moments of clarity Salaam had spoken about. Of course! He ought to take advantage of their being alone together to present Najeeb's plan to her and persuade her of the need to finance it. When Najeeb mentioned that plan to him, he had thought it unlikely to come to fruition. First, because of how strange it was, and also because of the need for some capital. But now, after seeing the money sitting a few steps in front of him, why not?

"May the Lord preserve him for me! He has buried me with gifts and money. 'Spend it, Mother,' he says to me. 'Live, and be happy! I have enough from what you spent on me through years of staying up late and slaving over the sewing machine or at the feet of customers.' I say to him, 'Enough, my dear! The house is full of boxes and other things.' Instead of one of everything, I came to have two, and sometimes more! Two televisions, two refrigerators, and so many tape players, vacuum cleaners, iron, and fans. It was so much that I had to bring things down to store in the basement. I would ask him, 'Where did you get this?' And he'd answer, 'A lucky find! I came across it in the market for next to nothing.' People ask why I don't throw away the old furniture, and I laugh in my heart. If they only knew! It's because I'm getting the groom ready to get married and move to his new house where he'll have everything he needs..."

But why shouldn't Luqman take a shortcut and convince Salaam? Lurice wasn't a sure thing. Even if she understood him and gave him her word in this moment of lucidity, how could he be sure that she wouldn't forget again and make all his efforts with her go to waste?

"...Then he proposed to Salaam, and I insisted all the more: 'Your fiancée isn't a young woman of twenty, and if you don't hurry, I'm not going to get the grandchildren I deserve.' I would open my heart and beat my breast as I prayed for him: 'Oh, Lord, keep him safe! You are the one who had mercy upon me and gave him to me after all my vows and my waiting. Keep him safe from wicked people, and from evil, and from harm. Have mercy on him, just as he has mercy on the orphans, the widows, and the poor. He looks after them, distributing food and assistance to them.' And you, Luqman, aren't you going to come to your senses like your friend and find yourself a respectable bride?"

But of course! Salaam, the one busy setting the table in the kitchen, was Luqman's key to the guarded treasure.

CHAPTER 7

"What are you doing here? Don't you know evening visits are against the rules?"

"I'm not a visitor. I came to ask for permission for Najeeb to leave, and the director agreed. She's the one who told me to wait here while they finish gathering his things."

"Is he your brother?"

"Nearly. He's a close friend."

"Listen, if he leaves, he might start taking drugs again. And if he gets addicted a second time, he'll be sent straight to prison because, from now on, we won't take him in here. We made an exception and gave him a chance by keeping him here and giving him work. The director of the asylum took compassion on him after he begged and pleaded. So she entrusted him with the job of cleaning and polishing the dishes. And you, what do you do?"

"I'm a businessman."

"A businessman! What kind?"

"Cars."

"Really?"

The attendant stared at him in disbelief. Luqman jingled his car keys—Salaam's keys. "I forgot my cell phone in the car. Could I make a call?" he asked.

The attendant surveyed him dubiously. Then he pointed to the glass phone booth near the door. He stood up to listen in, as though putting Luqman to the test.

Luqman typed a number and began speaking in a loud voice, "Have you finished the customs forms? Good. And the inventory? Who? What did he want? No, no. Stolen cars are not my specialty. Tell him to look for another dealer. We run an honorable business, and we don't want any problems...I'll come by first thing tomorrow...Of course, I've postponed my trip for another few days."

The attendant was satisfied. Indeed, he was so satisfied and pleased that he offered to get Luqman a cup of coffee or some refreshments.

"Tell me, sir, which cars do you recommend?"

"Mercedes! No question about it. Mercedes is the queen of cars. Durable, economical, and spare parts are cheap and widely available. Take my word for it as God's own truth!"

"Do you deal in used cars?"

"New cars too. Why? Are you looking to buy?"

"I am. But I'm looking for something good. Something from the past few years, for instance."

"How will you pay?" Luqman asked. "I don't accept payment by installments."

"I'll take care of it," the attendant answered. "I've set aside some money."

"From your salary?"

"What salary, man? Are you making fun of me? Since when have state salaries paid for cars? No. During the war, when money was growing on trees, I was swimming in cash. The good Lord said, 'Here, take it,' and so I took an unbelievable share. Excuse me, they're calling for me."

Thank God he was free of that vile attendant. The next step would have been him asking for Luqman's telephone number, his home address, and the address of his car lot.

"By God, Najeeb is a gentleman! A prince! If only he didn't have a drug habit!"

Here comes another attack, thought Luqman. But less fierce because coming from a kid wearing striped pajamas that made him look like a zebra escaped from the zoo.

This other guy offered Luqman a cigarette, which he gratefully took after sitting down next to him in the reception hall.

"You're a car dealer, you say? Nice to meet you! I'm in the same business. Was, actually. My father is the one who put up the money. Hey, do you have any snow on you? Just a quick sniff, or are you...No, it's clear you're not a user. What's new on the outside?"

To avoid similar questions requiring answers, Luqman fired back, "And what are you doing in this state institution, given that your father is a big car dealer and financier?"

"No, don't get me wrong," the young man responded. "You are in the rich ward here! The ward of those who pay big bucks to call the shots in this country! Don't you see the comfort we are in? A television, a reception hall, smoking, playing cards, respect...To tell the truth, the only thing missing are some cooing doves—you know what I'm saying? And a cute, plump nurse or two. Just to enjoy ourselves."

"You mean to say there are two wings, one for the wealthy addicts and another for the poor?" Luqman asked in jest.

The young man clapped his hands together. "God Almighty! Here you go making the same mistake! According to the law, this department isn't supposed to discriminate between the poor and the rich, especially in anything connected to addiction. We're in a state-run sanatorium, aren't we? Listen, do you know what happens when the state arrests an addict?"

"It throws him in prison?" Luqman replied.

"You've seen the light! Exactly," the kid exclaimed. "It stuffs him in prison immediately. No doctors, and no one gets out. That's when they separate the wheat from the chaff. Anyone who has someone watching his back, or whose family has plenty of greenbacks—I'm talking about dollars—they sit at the right hand of the state and are transferred here with all due respect and reverence. The rest are thrown off to the left and rot in prison, trampled under the feet of the guards and the inmates, waiting for trials that will confirm their sentence of months or years. Now do you understand, buddy?"

Luqman laughed. Of course, he understood. That's how Najeeb got out of prison then. That's how he persuaded the director to keep him there, and why she gave him permission to leave. And that's how he spent all the money he had amassed.

Najeeb had never been addicted to drugs a day in his life. Luqman had always known that about him, and Najeeb had confirmed it when they met by chance during the previous visit. For who was like Najeeb in that profession? He had worked for years as a sniper, picking off dozens of men—hundreds. Yet he practiced his art in full clarity of mind and never, ever needed medicine or drugs.

"Okay, I leave you in God's hands. It's time for dinner. If you come back to visit, think about us a little, and you'll get something delightful that blows your mind... Here I come!" called the young man dressed in striped pajamas like a zebra as he set off in the direction of the attendant waiting for him in the door.

Luqman looked at his watch, wondering what in the world could be keeping Najeeb. Oh, well. He'd pass the time watching TV after the patients went off to dinner and the reception hall emptied out.

"...All such people ought to be isolated and to receive the harshest punishment. Otherwise, they'll corrupt society and future generations, completely ruining the morals of young people..."

"And how wonderful morals are, Madame Nidal!" shouted one of the inmates behind Luqman. "Indeed, and we are a people who cannot live without morals! We are a people with a true passion for morals!"

Luqman didn't turn around to identify where the voice was coming from or to make the acquaintance of the speaker. He had no desire for more conversation, so he kept his eyes fixed on the television screen.

The broadcaster, "Madame Nidal," continued her discussion of the topic of homosexuality and sexual perversion. A legal scholar was agreeing with her, clarifying that "the law knows very well how to deal with these degenerate, depraved, and dissolute perverts, and how to bring upon their heads the most severe penalties."

A young doctor was nodding his head enthusiastically while the views of the Madame President of the Council for Thought exceeded all expectations: "Life in prison, forced labor, the diseases that come with sexual perversion and deviancy..."

"We have a Council for Thought, people," proclaimed the voice, "and it has a president who proves that humans are descended from monkeys!"

Why the racket, fucker? Luqman was thinking. Where did this madman come from? And why didn't he go have dinner with the others? Whew! The program finally finished, and here is Nidal signing off and introducing the news broadcast.

"A young man and his sister, in the prime of their youth, were found dead..." said the news anchor.

"A new type of corpse, made in our era of peace," echoed the voice.

"God! This day is not going to end well," whispered Luqman.

The newscaster continued, "They were coming home after visiting their sick father in the hospital. When they entered the house, they surprised a thief who was startled and swung around with his pistol and..."

"Bam, bam!" barked the voice, completing the sentence.

"Goddamn your father to hell this very night!" thought Luqman.

"We'll be right back after a short commercial break," said the anchor.

A rising male star with slicked hair appeared, standing on stage, rocking and swaying, at a party that took place every Saturday night until dawn, at some restaurant...

"Yes, these are morals, you cunts!" commented the voice. "Parties costing enormous sums in restaurants that are transformed into brothels. And why? To listen to singers singing like I shit and piss..."

Luqman remained silent, listening to a second commercial, in which the television promised viewers that the building standing proudly on the seashore was a unique creation, the likes of which had never been seen before: "...we can bring our yacht into its marina and leave it there. Then we go right up in our swimming suits, if we want, to our magnificent apartment that is bigger than a palace..."

"Oh, yes! These are morals, you whore!" roared the voice, as though still talking to Madame Nidal. "A building where we park 'our yacht.' We, who still, in war or in peace, carry drinking water from the bottom of our buildings up to the top floor since our faucets squeak but nothing comes out. These are morals, you dogs—petty thefts, murders, and general decline. God! The cock of the biggest queer in the world has more honor than your pretty faces, you lowlifes, you criminals!"

Luqman burst out in laughter. He couldn't hold it in. A queer, maybe, but tough! Yes, shout aloud! Raise your voice! Wipe them all out, every single one! Indeed, they deserve much more than that. They—

Najeeb arrived, breathing heavily. He couldn't believe his eyes when he saw Luqman applauding a sick man who stood on a chair, screaming and shouting curses.

"Keep it down!" Najeeb told him. Then he hurriedly pulled Luqman along by the arm to get them out before they attracted attention and came to some bad end.

CHAPTER 8

"Lukman, baby! I mees you very much!"

"Do you see? This is the Communista!" Luqman said to Najeeb, as he let Marina into the dim apartment, lit by candles. He took the bottle of whiskey from her hand, as well as the appetizers and main dishes she had purchased. Then he looked at his friend and asked, "Well, what do you think?"

"What do I think?" answered Najeeb. "First, give me a glass, man, and I'll be happy to tell you everything I think."

Luqman went into the kitchen and came back with three glasses. He poured a glass for himself and for Najeeb. Marina ate; the other two ate and drank. When Najeeb's tongue was loosened, he asked, "How long have you known languages?"

Luqman laughed. "Instead, you tell me how long has this"—he made an obscene gesture—"needed any talking? Do you see me passing my time with her in conversation?"

Marina asked them what they were saying, but they didn't respond. In the end, she got up, announcing she was very full and was going into the bedroom to lie down and rest for a while.

Luqman got up and took out some candles to replace the ones that had melted down and gone out. Najeeb asked him, "Are things really that bad?"

"Not any longer," answered Luqman as he took out of his pocket a stack of hundred-dollar bills. "Tomorrow, I'll pay the electricity bill. I'll toss out all this furniture you see. I'll bring in workers to clean, repair, and paint everything. You'll see! Two weeks at most, and you won't recognize this apartment. By the way, let's go to the market tomorrow to buy everything we need. Najeeb, we're through with this filth and deprivation. We'll bring back the good old days once again. God willing, we'll put this poverty behind us once and for all!"

Najeeb smiled. "Those were the days, weren't they? If only the Albino were still alive, the gang would be complete."

Luqman frowned.

"I didn't mean it," Najeeb went on. "You're right. He's dead and we're still here...Luqman, do you remember that night we spent together in that village...What was its name?"

Luqman smiled.

"It doesn't matter. How long it's been since we had

fun like that! And the girl?"

"Nahla," said Luqman.

"Right, Nahla! To this day I've never understood why she died."

"Why she killed herself, you mean," said Luqman.

"She died, she killed herself—same difference. Don't tell me she was a virgin. All we wanted was a little fun, but there are some people who always turn fun into a tragedy. Isn't she the one who smiled at us and began winking and gesturing? Isn't she the one who came to us wanting it, without any pressure or threats? Did we lure her with money? Did we tempt her with gifts or promises? And when we began having some fun, she began resisting, saying no, and playing hard to get."

"Until you hit her," said Luqman.

"If I hadn't, she wouldn't have given in and gone along, and we wouldn't have been able to satisfy her with fondling and kissing and—"

"And searing her with a lighter," interrupted Luqman.

"Have you ever tasted a grilled nipple, Luqman? A divine thing, a rare flavor, a scent that pierces through to your heart and intoxicates your soul. I didn't mean her any harm, believe me. When we had gone to sleep, and I woke up and heard a creaking in the kitchen, I said to myself, 'How generous of her to make us coffee or breakfast as her own special way of expressing how grateful and indebted she feels.' The whore! I never thought she was searching the drawers for something to hang herself with at dawn...

"Do you hear what I'm saying, Luqman? I swear on my life, I've never felt lust like that, or the arousal and pleasure I felt that night. To this day, the taste of her nipples is still on my tongue. That's why I always took refuge in her memory whenever depression came over me."

--

Luqman wiped the dripping sweat from his body with a towel. Then he stood at the window, smoking a cigarette and thinking. He ought to install an air conditioner; otherwise the customers would suffocate in the stifling heat.

Customers! Such a beautiful thought—especially the ladies. Tomorrow, he'd make a list of the tools and supplies he needed. Then he'd go to the newspaper. No, it was still too early for an advertisement. He ought to finish preparing the office beforehand. He also needed to set up a phone, or entrust Salaam to deal with that and just buy a cell phone he could carry as an additional means of doing business.

But how would he determine the cost of the service? No matter what happened, he would require that customers paid in US dollars. He didn't want the local currency. That matter was settled, at least. The profits, too, still had to be lucrative even after he divided them with his partners, Najeeb and Salaam. And why shouldn't he take half, seeing as he provided the apartment? Salaam would say she was the one who provided the capital, even if it was Lurice who was the source of the money. The bitch, she made him sign papers and deeds that guaranteed her rights to the capital and to her share of the returns. Oh, well. He'd look into that later, given that he'd be in charge of the accounting and budgeting. He'd pay a small bribe here and there. He'd expense the right amount of bills and embezzle a little without—

Najeeb entered the room and came over to stand nearby. He took a cigarette from Luqman, lit it, and leaned against the windowsill as he smoked. "Man!" he said. "It's as though we're in hell! All these clouds and not a breath of wind...Hey, Luqman! There's a man in the street looking at us."

"Don't worry. He's a policeman."

"Since when did this end-times city put police back on the street?"

"Ever since peace came back, and the people of the neighborhood brought a petition to the local police station complaining of all the assaults and thefts."

Luqman left the window and went over to sit on the couch. Najeeb turned to face him, thinking something over, and said, "By the way, that Marina is out of this world. It's as though I haven't slept with a real woman in years."

"And the director—are you forgetting her?"

"God save me! If you only knew the things that whore made me do for her to keep me in the asylum! Not to change the subject, but what is it that's kept you up till now?"

"How do you expect me to sleep when I have three

guests in my bed—you, Marina, and your snoring, which is so loud that the walls shake!"

Najeeb smiled, "Sorry. Go in and sleep now, if you want. I'll stay out here and maybe lie down on the couch if I get very tired."

Luqman had a question in mind that had been bothering him ever since running into Najeeb. "Tell me, Najeeb. What is it that brought you to that institution if you weren't using drugs?"

"I was charged with addiction because the penalty for that was lighter than it was for dealing. When the war ended, I had no skills apart from my job as a sniper, so I told myself I would learn a new profession. It happened that I came across a big dealer who won me over, and I started working."

"How did they arrest you?"

"I was doing a buy at a house that got raided. They had me in prison in a heartbeat. If my dealer hadn't been a big shot, I mean, if he hadn't had friends in the government, I'd be pushing up daisies now. He was the one who took care of things and had the charges changed from dealing to using. Then he interceded on my behalf, I was transferred to the asylum, and...and you know the rest, right?"

Luqman nodded. Indeed, he knew the rest, but there was one last thing he needed to clarify. "Look, Najeeb, I'm trusting you. I've provided the capital, offered my apartment as the office, and made you partners with me and Salaam. Don't you think you ought to pay me back by explaining to me where you acquired all this science, with you being shut away with the mentally ill and the crazies?"

Najeeb said, "All this science came to me from a certain guy.

"He had been in the asylum for years by the time I got there. Of all the patients, he was the most famous, and everyone called him 'Einstein.' They told me his story and how he'd pay his children to catch rats for him. He gathered rats and worked with them until his apartment had been transformed into a laboratory overflowing with rodents. The building's tenants filed a complaint about him, and the police came. When they saw how old and knowledgeable he was, and that he was from a good family, they brought him to the mental institution.

"That's how I met him. We grew closer after I learned he had lost his children in the war, and when I saw how old he was. 'So, he has no heir,' I said to myself. 'Why don't I play the role of a son as long as he likes me and trusts me.' Then, by the time I realized that the will of a crazy or mentally disturbed person wouldn't be legally binding, I had gotten to know him, and a deep friendship had grown between us.

"He asked me to gather some rats for him, which I did, and he paid me. The institution's kitchen was full of rats. I nearly died of disgust. He was an old man full of weird stories that would make your hair stand on end.

"He kept on repeating that the rats were the ones who caused the war, until in the end he convinced me. It was as though I had no prior knowledge or any connection to all that had happened. It was as though I was innocent of that war. I would join with him in saying, 'It was the rats who caused the war and destroyed our lives. If it weren't for them, today I would be a farmer or a simple teacher with a wife and kids...'

"I don't know how to explain it to you, Luqman. I believed him. He persuaded me. Maybe because those things he would say offered me proof of my innocence. In my free time, I started visiting him and listening to his delusions for hours on end."

"Where is he today?" Luqman asked.

"He died," answered Najeeb. "The director sent for me and told me he had fallen ill with some kind of poisoning. She said that when the foam was bubbling from his mouth and he struggled against death, he was holding onto two notebooks, fiercely clutching them to his chest like someone clinging to a life preserver. And when the doctor arrived, and several of them tried to pull the notebooks away by force, the old man pulled the director close and whispered in her ear, 'Give them to Najeeb.'

"The director didn't understand, and neither did I. When we began flipping through the pages, we figured out that he had recorded in them all the information he had gathered about rats. The director laughed and said to me, 'Congratulations! This is your inheritance from Einstein.'

"I didn't laugh, myself. I took the thick notebooks with a kind of fear and awe, just to annoy her. Then I left her office, intending to toss them out. I don't know what stopped me from doing that. Maybe it was his constant talk about the rats having caused the war, or his delusions that made me imagine, at least for a moment, that those whom I had killed had only been animals. Or maybe it was that he was thinking of me like a beloved son in the last moment before the spirit left him..."

Najeeb stopped. He left the room, only to come back a few moments later with two notebooks. "Here they are."

Luqman took them in his hands. Two volumes in black leather, thick pages filled with beautiful, ornate handwriting.

"What are all these drawings and foreign symbols?"

"Just read the first notebook," Najeeb replied. "That's where he recorded in Arabic everything he observed about rats—their behavior, their habits, their physical characteristics. The second includes foreign expressions because it contains chemistry equations, recipes, and instructions about ways to combat them. There are also lists enumerating the types of traps, illnesses, poisons, materials, germs."

Najeeb took his leave and went into the bedroom to lie down. He was tired after such a long day.

--

Despite how late it was, Luqman's eyes still rejected sleep. That's the way Luqman was. Whenever someone slept beside him or occupied his living space, sleep eluded him. It was as though drowsiness were a fixed quantity of oxygen. If someone else consumed it, it was gone. So Luqman would lose his share of the sleep, being rendered a wide-eyed insomniac.

Luqman lit another candle. He lay on his back and took out a cigarette. Then he brought the notebook up to the light and began to read.

"There is a rat for every human on the face of the earth. But in our county, after the war, I estimate their number to be twenty-to-one. There are two types:

"*Rattus rattus*: It is also known as the black rat or the house rat. It originally comes from the Far East. It made its way to the Middle East on account of commerce and trade. Wherever it settles down, it brings the bubonic plague. It lives for three or four years. It makes its nests in house attics. It eats meat but prefers fruit and vegetables.

"*Surmulot ou rattus norvegicus*: It is known as the Norwegian rat (taking its name from the country where its existence was noticed for the first time), or else the gray rat or the migrant rat. It is bigger and fiercer than the black rat. Active at night. It lives hidden under the earth, in canals, in sewers, in all kinds of places and environments. It feeds on corpses, both human and animal, on plants, and on small, living prey. It gnaws on everything to find nourishment, even metal, paper, rubber, and cloth. The male is violent, engaging in ferocious battles. They eat each other when hungry. The strong will jump on the weak, open their skulls, eat their brains, and afterwards the rest of the body and limbs. It is the strongest, most dangerous, and most widespread type. It kills the black rat."

Luqman raised his eyes from the notebook. That one he had seen in the bathroom window—what type was it? And the other one that bedded down in Salaam's oven? In any case, if it were permissible to make a comparison between rats and people, then he, Najeeb, and the Albino would be the superior Norwegian species.

"The rat is present in every corner of the earth. It loves temperate climates, secure dwellings, and abundant food. It fights for survival with enormous tenacity, and it has the temperament of a traveler or vagabond...

"It reaches sexual maturity two months after being born. It mates in all seasons, with all females. Rats multiply rapidly since the female is pregnant more than ten times a year for a period of twenty days. In each litter, it can birth up to twenty young."

Now you're talking! It mates in all seasons and with all females! Do you hear that, Partner? If I were a rat, we'd never be idle, and I'd find you a suitable bride every day. I'd be the master, and I'd gather all the females in a harem for you and for me.

"The rat is the most destructive, the most gluttonous, and the most reproductive animal. It doesn't kill just when it is hungry, but also, and especially, because it enjoys destruction. Nothing it eats can make it vomit.

"It is classified as a rodent because its teeth never stop growing. Therefore, in order to halt their growth, it constantly bites, gnaws, and digs with its teeth. It can fall from a great height and not be hurt at all. It can jump up to three feet or more in the air. When cornered, they become fierce and may jump, bite, and inflict wounds.

"Its memory is prodigious. It passes on information about a specific poison from generation to generation, for instance. Rats that live in the city are cleverer than those in the country because they acquire more experience.

"It is nocturnal, and if it appears in the light of day, that means the population has become enormous, leading to food shortages. In their movements, rats keep close to the walls because their eyesight is weak. In that way, it is safe from danger on one side. They always follow the same track.

"It lives in groups, or tribes, but it enjoys the feeling of being big and independent. If it senses danger, it is able to organize armies and send out hordes, the savagery of which surpasses everything that is recorded about the Berbers or the Tatars. Tribes may sometimes attack individuals of their own species, killing and laying waste. Females and the young are not spared these ferocious battles and wars.

"Its essential vices are four, not seven, like the vices of humans, insofar as they do not know sloth, envy, and pride. They are characterized by gluttony, lust, greed, and wrath.

"It enjoys powerful nationalistic sentiments and is noted for a deep hatred towards outsiders and strangers, even from their own species. If a stranger joins a group, it is left alone to wander around for a while until it begins to feel safe and pushes into the middle. That's when the tribe gathers around it. With bulging eyes, and squeaking with high, sharp, heart-rending voices, they begin to tear, shred, and rip.

"Only two kinds of living creatures make war against their own species: the rat and the human. These two do not benefit any other living creatures, and they destroy all types of life."

Only a flicker of life remained in the last candle Luqman had lit. Its wick leaned a little. It trembled with a final blaze before sinking into a quagmire of melted wax that flowed down to congeal on the small table where Luqman had tossed the notebook. Darkness reigned, and his internal clock indicated the morning was only a few steps away.

CHAPTER 9

Salaam was nervous.

The director didn't usually call her into his office. He would usually summon the rest of the women in the Central, especially the young and pretty ones, whether they were married or not. And when it was someone's turn to go in to see him, the others would note the time and begin winking and whispering until she came out again. Then they would gather around her, with jokes and laughter spreading through the group.

Salaam smoothed her skirt. Then, with a bit of pride, she headed for the director's office, looking at the other women with sidelong glances, as though her time had finally come after a long and patient suffering. She knocked on the door and was invited in. She went in and remained standing. The director stood up to greet her with a warm welcome. He asked her to take a seat, and he sat nearby, doing away with formalities.

Salaam relaxed.

The director began by insisting she light a cigarette and have something hot or cold to drink, all the while looking at her knees, which the hem of her skirt pulled back to reveal, with eyes that gleamed with lust and speculation. When she kept on refusing, he smiled.

The director leaned back in his chair and said, "You are the most senior woman we have, Ms. Salaam. I hope you are as happy to remain with us as we are to have you."

What was going through his head, Salaam wondered. Was he finally remembering her after all the other girls had visited him, and he had been dissatisfied with them? Or did he have some plan in mind? In any case, no matter his intentions, this surprising visit was a win. When she left, she would act exactly like all the others. She would walk slowly, with a certain coquetry, leaning her head back to shake out her hair. She didn't have hair to shake out, but no problem. She would find some other gesture, no less suggestive, and she'd let out a moaning sigh, a little like a meow.

After some general conversation on this and that to get things going, the director said, "Miss Salaam, you are far and away the most qualified and experienced woman working here. Therefore, after a long and careful consideration, I have decided to put you in change of the others. Of course, this means an increase in pay, in rank, and in standing. But an increase in responsibility and duties, too."

Salaam was annoyed.

She found it strange how, instead of jumping up in joy, she felt the blood rising to her face and throbbing in her temples and ears.

"And the other manager?" she asked with some emotion. She knew this question of hers didn't come from any concern or pang of conscience, but from an urgent need to grab onto some life preserver before sinking further under that emotion.

"Poor woman!" the director responded. "I don't know what clouded her judgment so much that she would go around paying for things with bad checks. Just today, I was informed that she would be held by the district attorney while waiting for them to conduct further investigations.

"I don't know what comes over people! Last week, the police came one morning to arrest my neighbor, the bank employee. Embezzlement! People are no longer satisfied with their lot in life.

"What did our woman here have to complain of, seeing as she was a government employee with a respectable salary and a secure job? Do you think she dressed like she did and spent like she did from her salary alone? I don't mean anything bad by saying this, but what I mean is that I used to overlook the gifts and bribes she used to pocket on the side."

Salaam understood.

What the director was offering her was the following: if she played the role of spying on the other women, she could cheat people on the price of calls and ask for more money in exchange for providing better service. And the proceeds? She'd divide them with him, of course, each according to the importance of his position.

The director smiled and said flirtatiously, "Nothing kills me like a smart woman." He reached over to shake hands so as to congratulate her and encourage further cooperation and success.

Salaam turned around before going out the office door and said, "The mother of my deceased fiancé, may he rest in peace, doesn't have anyone else to look after her, and..."

"I understand," answered the director. "You can leave in the afternoon. Today you'll only work half a shift. This is a gift to you and an expression of my great confidence in our partnership, which I hope will be fruitful and loyal to the end."

--

Salaam stood in front of the window at the sandwich shop and ordered: "One shwarma, one falafel, and one chicken. With lots of garlic, please!"

She would eat out of anger. She would bite, chew, swallow, and drink until she choked. Maybe food would calm her down. The animals! All men were animals! Stupid, foolish, and loathsome, strutting about like mindless roosters. As soon as they see a butt, a leg, or a piece of naked flesh, they open their mouths, breath panting and tongues hanging out like hungry, horny dogs that jump on anything.

And the women? Whores! All of them, without exception. And she, what would she do in this corrupted, wretched world? A woman like her deserved a better man—the very best, by God! Goddamn you, Albino, did you have to die? Wasn't it possible for you to marry me first? To put the ring on my finger, and then to go off to depths of hell, if that's what you wanted? Wasn't a solitary widow better than a spinster no man would turn to look at? And that bastard, Luqman, that lowlife sponge, who cared only about money! And the director—with all these males around me, he was the last thing my life needed. All of you can go and die. I'll cry over the lot of you and publicize an eternal period of mourning.

Salaam arrived at the funeral services shop.

The old man wasn't alone. Salaam preferred to wait outside, hoping he wouldn't take too long with the female customer. She leaned against a car parked nearby, keeping the old man and his customer in her line of sight through the window.

She watched the two of them debating. They wandered slowly between the coffins. They would stop for a few seconds, then continue their circuit. The old man's face began to betray something like resentful disgust. Salaam smiled. The customer had to be haggling with him about the cost. Now they were retreating into the recesses of the shop, which meant they were dropping off in price. Top-of-the line styles and the best quality were put in the front of the shop near the door. Older and cheaper models were stacked in the back.

The customer scratched her head and sweated. Anguish was clear on her face. Anguish, mixed with some embarrassment or confusion, as though the old man were addressing her with utter contempt, rebuking her, or characterizing her in the most insulting way.

A horn blared behind Salaam. She jumped and turned around to watch a car speeding by as fast as a bullet. She poured out a bucket of abuse on the driver. She turned back to the shop. She saw that the old man was alone and cursing in his native language.

"Comes in, Madame Salaam," he said to her. "What have these days comes to? The customer wants a coffin, but not to spend her money! She can buy from somebody else. I am not a charity! Last week, a customer asks to lease her a coffin. She says, 'I take it for twenty-four hours, and after the burial ceremony, I bring it back.' Can you believe? Enough! No respect for the dead in this country. They put them in coffins made from the wood of vegetable crates, and then hoppa! Into the dirt you go! No funeral ceremony, no procession, no mourners. What do you expect from people who no longer mourn their dead, eh? And what do you hope for from a town that wastes boatfulls of money on junk and scrimps on the cost of giving its sorrow a dignified appearance? I'm sorry, Madame Salaam. Please to sit and rest. Do you want tea or coffee?"

Salaam thanked the old Armenian for the cup of coffee. Then she paid the price of the bronze plaque she had commissioned him to make. And when she was intending to leave, he said to her, "If you want me to hang an advertisement for your company in my storefront, you be my guest."

Salaam thanked him and went out to the street. The old man followed her out to say, "I folded the screws up in a small piece of paper, which I taped to the back of the plaque. Be careful not to lose them, Madame!"

--

The doorman said in his weird accent, "The electricity is out and the generator is broken, but Luqman is here. His colleague arrived a little while ago. God, what's his name?"

Salaam thought, "God, seven flights! With the dark stairwells and the rats!"

The doorman looked at her as though reading her thoughts and said, "Adnan, take the lamp and go up with the lady."

Salaam didn't thank him, even though he had called her lady when he usually just called the tenants by their first names without adding a "mister" or a "sir." She didn't thank him because she knew that the son of the doorman (who was called Abu Adnan, given that his son's name was Adnan) would only go up with her to Luqman's apartment with the expectation that she pay him, as though he were a taxi driver dropping off his passengers.

Salaam banged on the door with her fist, gasping for breath as her chest heaved. She waited a few seconds, and when there was no answer, she kicked the door with every ounce of strength she had.

Luqman opened the door, glowering and ready to let fly a string of abuse. But he was surprised to see Salaam, exhausted from the heat and the exertion. The color of her face had changed to a greenish-purple. The sweat had made her appearance even more ugly and out of sorts than usual.

"Sorry! I didn't hear you," he said. He brought her in, looking at the package wrapped in paper that she was carrying. "What is this?" he asked her.

She extended the plaque to him and replied, "A gift!"

Luqman smiled. He quickly cut the string and tore off the wrapping paper. But his face soon fell when he discovered the bronze plaque. In order to conceal his reaction from her watchful eyes, he turned and called, "Najeeb! Come, see what Salaam brought us!"

Najeeb came out of the office with a tired look and dirty clothes. Salaam had never seen him like this before. She looked at him curiously until he said by way of explanation, "Work clothes. I got back just now from an assignment in a big commercial warehouse."

"In that case, the work must be going as well as can be," she said, looking for more information.

Luqman corrected, "Don't get ahead of yourself, Salaam. It was an order that came in after weeks of waiting."

"Don't worry. They'll call," she returned. "There are more rats in this town than there are people. You'll see!"

Najeeb took the bronze plaque from Luqman's hand and read aloud.

S.L.N. Associates
Rat Extermination

He asked, "What does this name mean?"

Salaam replied, "They are the first letters of our names, the three of us."

Najeeb: "Why did you use Western letters?"

Salaam: "Because that looks more serious."

Luqman: "And why didn't you call it L.S.N., for example?"

Najeeb: "Grow up, man!"

Luqman: "What's wrong with you two? Can't you tell a joke anymore?"

Salaam: "On my honor, you weren't joking. You're mad because I didn't put the letter of your name first!"

Luqman: "First of all, keep your voice down."

Salaam: "And second?"

Luqman: "And second, don't play games with me. Your intentions are as clear as day!"

Salaam: "My intentions? And what are my intentions?"

Luqman: "To make the two of us understand that you are in charge of this business, and that we are your employees! Remember where the capital came from, Salaam. Don't force me to get all the papers out!

Salaam: "All this, instead of thanking me for everything I've done and keep on doing for your sake, Luqman?"

Luqman: "Don't play the role of victim with me! If you didn't have an interest in doing otherwise, you'd let dogs tear me up and eat me alive. Do you think your talk about honor, principles, and morals can fool me?"

Salaam: "You're right. I deserve all this abuse and more. But there's one thing I know, Luqman. The times are changing and so is Salaam!"

Luqman: "Don't threaten me! We're finished. Consider the company dissolved from this moment on!"

Salaam: "Do you think I'm stupid, or just an idiot? Do you think I don't understand your game? You want to dissolve the company now, after everything? After you took the money, and after all we spent on buying the permit and the materials, on renovating your apartment, and on paying your rent and your overdue bills from over a year? Have you forgotten you were living for months by candlelight? Have you forgotten you were threatened with eviction from this apartment? Have you—"

Luqman: "Oh, my fucking God, Salaam! Just let it go! And if you don't..."

Salaam: "And if I don't, then what? Eh, Luqman? Tell me! If not, then what?"

The telephone rang. Luqman had been waiting for such an opportunity to extricate himself from the dispute and went into the office.

Najeeb said, "It'll be okay, Miss Salaam. We're all tired."

"You and I are tired, sure," Salaam followed. "But

him, what's making him tired? Can you explain to me what Master Luqman does all day long? He sits behind his desk waiting for phone calls? If receiving telephone calls was the only reason we needed the office, why did we need to pour so much money into renovating the apartment and replacing the furniture? The truth is, he's making a mockery out of you and me! He sits, relaxing in the air-conditioned room, ordering fast food and playing solitaire. Truly, very tiring stuff—no, exhausting!"

Luqman returned to the living room. He was frowning, and he was holding a small piece of paper on which he had recorded some address. Speaking to Najeeb, he said, "A customer called. He wants us to come to his apartment for an inspection."

Najeeb: "Now? I just returned a little while ago, and..."

Luqman: "I'll go. I'll see what the problem is. I'll consider the options, explain the cost, and come back. If he agrees on the price, we'll go back tomorrow together."

Najeeb: "And who will stay in the office?"

Luqman: "Don't worry about it. We'll look into that tomorrow. The solution is a cell phone."

Salaam: "Do you have any idea what it costs? About a thousand dollars, Mr. Luqman!"

He didn't answer her. He didn't even look at her. As though she were an insect. A chair. Some inanimate object. He said something in the direction of Najeeb as he went towards the front door. He grabbed the jacket hanging on the hook and went out. The door slammed behind him.

Najeeb remained standing in the middle of the room, looking at Salaam. In her rage, she had begun fanning her flushed face with her hands.

Najeeb said gently, "As long as the electricity is cut off during the day and comes back only at night, I might as well just get rid of the air conditioner. Perhaps the solution is to buy a generator."

When he saw how furious she was, he added, "This heat is going to kill someone if it keeps being cloudy and stifling like this."

As though suddenly remembering he was there, Salaam looked at him and asked, "When will Luqman return?"

Najeeb responded that when he was there to cover the office, Luqman took his time.

Salaam raised her eyebrows. Not bad, she thought. Without saying it directly, Najeeb is letting me know that he's on my side in my war with Luqman. "And does he often stay out late?" she asked.

Najeed replied, "That depends on whether he visits Marina or not."

"Marina?" screamed Salaam, as though bitten by a snake. "And who is this Marina?"

Najeeb was nonplussed, and he hastened to fix the situation by saying, "I don't know...I didn't say anything... If Luqman knew I mentioned her name in front of you, he'd kill me...If I tell you who she is, will you promise not say anything?"

After he had told her about Luqman's relationship with Marina, Salaam stood up and went over to the window, trying to get more air. Najeeb looked at her back, and a half smile appeared on the corners of his mouth. The smile immediately turned to a pensive frown when she turned around. Salaam began staring as though she had suddenly happened upon the thread that would guide her to a valuable treasure.

Salaam didn't need it to be spelled out for her that Luqman and Marina weren't the important ones in the story, but that Najeeb had something else in mind. And Najeeb didn't need more conversation to be certain that his hook had been well cast, and that he just needed to wiggle it a few more times, and this spinster, stuffed with money, would swallow it. Nothing in the world was easier than catching a woman in love on a hook baited with her own jealousy for another woman. And there was nothing easier than seducing Salaam, whose desire overwhelmed her like a fish being thrown up on the sand by the waves.

Najeeb slowly undid the buttons of his shirt. "Excuse me," he said, rubbing the thick, intertwined hair on his chest, "I'm going in to take a shower."

Salaam swallowed the saliva that gathered in the bottom of her mouth as soon as she saw his bare chest. She made a move as though intending to leave, but he grabbed her by the arm to stop her. He poured into her eyes a look charged with suggestion. He took her hand and put it on his chest. His beating heart pumped a poison that flowed through her limbs and made her shiver like a bird about to be slaughtered.

He took her to the bathroom. He sat in the bathtub and asked her to take the soap in her hand and run it over his entire body. Salaam obeyed. She began to lather his limbs slowly, leisurely, meticulously, submissively, as though she were taking the time to explore his body, getting to know one part after another.

He brought her out and stood her in the middle of the room. When he lashed her back, her neck, her thighs, her hands and feet, her breasts, and her face with his leather belt, she didn't scream. She didn't even moan. She twisted a little as though a gentle hand were spanking her tenderly. It didn't frighten her to see purplish-red lines criss-crossing her body, and his hand didn't make her jump when it reached up to pull her head back by the hair and force her onto her knees.

The more submissive she was, the more aroused Najeeb became. He rewarded her by throwing her to the ground and collapsing on top of her. He began to knock her head against the floor and spitting on her, increasing his pleasure by shouting out the obscene things.

"Salaam!" Najeeb groaned out and flopped on his back as he tried to catch his breath. His chest rose and fell with the speed of an animal fleeing from a hunter's rifle.

Salaam opened her eyes. She wanted to scream out loud, to trill, to rejoice, to shout, "Bravo, Salaam! See how you've been rewarded after waiting so long!" But she suppressed that desire of hers and grabbed something to wipe off the blood that dripped from her nose and mouth onto her chest and stomach.

Salaam looked with pride and wonder at the stallion stretched out beside her on the floor and said flirtatously, "I hope you enjoyed yourself. Next time, don't forget to enter me through the front door. For something you may not know is that I am still sealed by the red wax of my virginity."

CHAPTER 10

This doorman didn't have a weird accent, and he didn't particularly look like that other doorman either.

With perfect politeness, he respectfully asked Luqman's name and his business before inviting him to sit in one of the leather chairs scattered around the foyer. The doorman lifted the telephone receiver and said, "Miss Shireen, Mr. Luqman has arrived." He was silent for two or three seconds, and then he said, "Mr. Luqman, Miss Shireen is waiting for you. It's the fourth floor, the apartment on the left."

Luqman stood, waiting for the elevator. He could have taken the stairs, but he decided deep down that people of a certain social status calmly waited for the elevator.

A woman came up, holding a boy's hand. She greeted Luqman. "Good morning," she said in English. She entered the elevator, and he followed her in. Her finger went to the button for the sixth floor, and she uttered a sentence that he didn't understand. He nodded his head, smiling and hiding feelings of distress. She pressed the button, and the elevator started going up. The clean, blond boy smiled and lifted the toy he was carrying to show it to Luqman. The elevator arrived at the sixth floor. The lady said thanks and disappeared. Luqman pressed the button for the eighth floor so as to give her the impression he understood what she had said and was just heading to a floor above hers.

He arrived at the eighth floor, but he didn't open the door, nor did he push the button for the fourth floor. The elevator's electric light went out. Luqman closed his eyes and felt his heart beating furiously, which was entirely out of character. "What's wrong with you?" he asked himself. It's no doubt that smell. The smell of a surprising perfume. It wasn't luxurious or pleasing in the clear sense of the word, nor easily defined like spices or flowers. A light scent, unrevealing. Nothing over the top, but subdued. It whispers deliberately, and by the time you are paying attention to it, it has already penetrated you and taken up residence.

Luqman opened his eyes. What in the world was waiting for him on the fourth floor? Miss Shireen! He hadn't told Najeeb and Salaam that the customer was a woman who had a beautiful voice and spoke in a strange accent. As soon as he heard that voice in the telephone receiver, his anger had vanished like water poured over him that ran right off his skin.

Luqman pushed the elevator door partway open, and the light came back on. He turned around to a big mirror and stood looking at himself. If only he had taken a shower before coming. Or at the very least, if only he had put on some cologne. He wet his fingers with saliva and ran them through his hair to slick it back. He adjusted the collar of his jacket. Luqman raised an eyebrow and frowned. No! It would be better to smile a little, with a hint of a frown. "Not bad at all, Mr. Luqman," he said to himself. Then he looked at his hairy chest where a chain was hanging down. He breathed in deeply and exhaled, holding in his stomach to hide the small potbelly that had begun to protrude somewhat. Luqman thought he needed a little exercise to take care of any negative effects of his thirty-eight years.

"It's nice to meet you, Miss Shireen," he said aloud and with an aggressive self-confidence. But he soon decided that his shirt had too many buttons open to tempt a woman with a name like this. How old was she? Was she blond or dark? Blond, definitely. Tall and alluring, but without any vulgarity. Her voice revealed all that. Well, what do you think, Partner? If she actually is as you imagine and expect, if my guess hits the mark, and she is splendid, lovely, and well born, promise me you'll keep your head to demonstrate that you, too, had a good upbringing.

The elevator suddenly started going down, and Luqman knew that someone at the bottom must have summoned it. Luqman pressed the stop button, and then the button for the fourth floor. Meanwhile, he quickly buttoned his shirt up and hid his necklace inside it. He had intended to leave the last button open, but fate decreed to pop off one of his middle buttons, the one over his stomach, to be precise. It flew up against the mirror, bounced off, and fell into the small crack between the floor and the elevator door.

Now Luqman was standing in front of her door in a shirt open at the belly button. The last thing he needed! And what to do now? Turn on his heel and go back where he came from?

Luqman looked at the small white square to the side of the door and read her full name. Dear God, how could he leave a woman bearing a name like this without even having seen her? Goddamn her, who could she be? And since when had he, Luqman, feared the glances of women like her? Who could say she wasn't an old woman who retained only an aristocratic surname?

Luqman pushed the doorbell. He stood and waited. When he didn't hear a response, he pressed again, harder this time, until he saw a shadow cover the light of the peephole and the door opened.

She let him in quickly and apologized, running back to the other room because she was talking on the telephone. Luqman closed the door. He went down the hall, guided by her voice. He was annoyed by the sound of his worn-out sandals on the white marble, so he walked half on tiptoes in order to soften his footfalls.

He pressed on into the living room. He was surprised

by the amount of light pouring through the large glass window, opening to sea and sky. The few pieces of furniture, scattered here and there, were yellow and white. Plants, different levels, sofas low to the floor, and a large wooden trunk that was carved and inlaid with mosaics. A stereo playing soft music. Magazines and newspapers thrown on the floor. Files and papers piled up on a large table, which also had a computer that was turned on. Paintings with strange shapes and colors, a large vase filled with an enormous bouquet of flowers.

Luqman sat in the closest seat he found. It was very low. He crossed one leg over the other. His small paunch pressed out and made the absence of a button obvious. He decided to remedy the situation by closing his jacket even though it was hot. He wasn't comfortable in his position, so he shifted both feet back to the floor. He wondered about what to do with his hands. He thought about going to the chair near the table but changed his mind when he remembered his sandals and calculated the distance he would have to cover to reach it.

How uncomfortable and annoyed he was! He shouldn't have come. He should have stayed with Najeeb and Salaam. It's all your fault, Partner! You always entangle me by inventing stories and situations. Take a good look at her. Do you think a woman like her would turn to look at you or pay you any attention?

Kneeling near the big glass window, she was speaking French into the phone, mixing some Arabic words into her sentences. He hadn't been able to make out her features well in the dark hallway, and now he was unable to see anything except her back. She didn't have a large build. She walked around barefoot. She wore jeans and a white shirt that was much too big for her slender body.

Her thick, red hair was gathered on top of her head and held in place by a pencil. She reached up behind her head to find a strand that had escaped and push it in with the rest. The nape of her shining white neck came into view, flashing at him in the sunlight with a soft, blond fuzz, like a sparrow's downy feathers. Her hand remained, holding her neck as she moved her head back and forth. A small hand, a child's hand. Her fingers were neither fat nor skinny, but just as they should be. Her fingernails were short and unpainted.

Suddenly, she turned towards him and smiled. Then she went on speaking into the receiver.

She was wearing glasses! Small, round, thin glasses with metal frames anchored on her petite nose. Luqman couldn't believe his eyes. A young woman with glasses— what in the world! It was as though he had never seen something like this before. Or if he had, it was utterly unlike what he was seeing now.

She grew tired of her previous position, moving her head a little and sitting cross-legged on the floor. He saw a third of her face. He couldn't see her mouth, which was hidden behind her hand. She was biting her nails and frowning. No earrings. No bracelet or necklace. Just a small, round watch with a delicate black leather band. How old was she? In her early thirties. Or her late twenties. Somewhere in there, to be sure.

A woman like this makes a man desire to eat her, not to sleep with her, Luqman thought. Like a piece of hard candy, Turkish delight, or cotton candy. He would put her in his mouth, and instead of chewing, he would let her melt on his tongue to release her flavor slowly. Marina had her mint flavor. And Miss Shireen? Strawberry or orange. No, she wasn't a flavor, but an odor. Jasmine. That was it. She would spread through the room if the air moved her. She would blow away in silence, slowly, gently flowing back and forth on breezes intermingling like waves. Everything about her was different and unfamiliar. Her street, her doorman, her neighbor, her elevator, her name, her apartment, her accent, everything.

"I've kept you waiting. I'm sorry, but it was a work call."

Luqman didn't respond. He kept staring at her for a few seconds. Then, when she came over and stretched out her hand to shake, he stood up abruptly and greeted her warmly. She apologized again, saying she would turn off the computer and be all his in just a moment. The phrase pleased him: in just a moment she'd "be all his."

She went to the table. He remained standing and a certain embarrassment came over him until he put his hand in his pants pocket and turned to look at a painting hanging on the wall. In order to make conversation with her, he said, "It's a very beautiful painting. Did you make it?"

"*C'est une reproduction de Van Gogh. Elle vous plaît?*" Shireen answered in French, still staring at the computer screen.

Luqman wondered what he should answer now, given that he didn't understand a word she had said. From the music of her voice, he sensed she had asked him a question. His guess was confirmed when he saw her looking at him over her work table as though waiting for some response. He looked at her. Then he nodded and smiled while raising an eyebrow.

She smiled in turn as she figured out that he didn't understand French. In order to find a way out for herself and to put him at ease, she turned back to the computer screen and said, "You're making fun of me!"

Luqman took a deep breath to calm his heart after having safely passed that test. He decided to press the attack before she launched another loaded question. He said, "If you don't mind my asking, what kind of work do you do?"

She turned off the computer and stood up, asking him if he wanted a bit of Nescafé. Luqman said yes and thanked her. She invited him to come with her. That way, she could show him at the same time where she had seen the mouse.

Walking in front of him down the hallway to the kitchen, she said, "I work in archeological excavations. I came with a French delegation as part of a joint program between UNESCO and the Public Conservation Administration."

"Are you French?"

"Nearly. I was born here, but I emigrated with my father as a young girl as soon as the war broke out. This is the first time I've been back after being gone for twenty years."

"But you speak Arabic very well."

"Of course! It was my father, God bless his soul, who insisted on speaking to me in Arabic."

"Are you happy to be back?"

She turned to him, thinking it over, and a hint of sadness came over her face. While putting a pot of water on the burner, she said, "I don't know what to say, even though I've been here a few months. My father is the one who made me come back. I mean, I came back because of him in a certain sense. He dreamed his whole life of returning. Then he got sick and died a year before the end of the war."

Shireen's voice quivered, and Luqman noticed tears forming in her eyes that she tried to mask by going to the cupboard to get a couple cups.

"And you?" she asked. "What about you?"

Luqman was silent. A long, deep silence. He lowered his head and stared at the floor.

Shireen was embarrassed. "I didn't mean it," she said. She turned her head to look out the window as she sipped her cup of Nescafé.

Luqman wondered, What must she be thinking about me that she would feel this degree of guilt? She must be thinking I'm a victim of the war. That was it, no question. Me, a victim? If you only knew! Just a little while ago, after realizing that she was a secure fortress protected by a hundred walls, he had been wondering how he would ever get inside her. How nice that he hadn't given up too quickly, seeing how she, just like that and without any effort at all, had revealed her secret and surrendered the keys.

Some moments passed, after which Luqman raised his head from the floor with a troubled look and said, "If you would show me now what the problem is, Miss Shireen."

--

When Luqman left her place, he was a different man.

Of his entire history, he only kept his name. Luqman had been an only child when his parents died in the war. A car bomb exploded in front of their building, and they were among the victims. He had been away at the time, visiting one of his friends.

He left school and joined one of the factions. He fought for some years. Then, when he discovered that it was a war between interests, profiteers, and scoundrels, he left the militia. He tried to commit suicide numerous times, but luck hadn't been on his side. Then he came back to his senses and decided to fight to stay alive. He worked various odd jobs. Later, when the war ended, he and his friends went in together and decided to set up a rat extermination company.

Luqman spoke about politics, about principles, about the roots of the conflict. He wrapped up his discourse with a long oration on the lack of morals and on decline.

The fish, Shireen, nibbled the bait and was caught on his hook.

She would love him. Wasn't he a victim of the war to which her father had also been a victim, too, in a certain sense? Of course. She would love him in spite of herself, if it came to that. He would do everything in his power to make her fall in love with him, to make it impossible to do without him. Shireen was the hand that would blot out his past with the stroke of a pen, opening wide the doors of the future. She needed him. He wanted her. He needed the title, the position, and the social recognition. Hell, maybe she would even provide him with another citizenship and residence in a foreign country. Didn't she say she would be leaving after she finished her project here, that she'd return to her work in Paris? Paris! Oh, blessed and glorious day sent by God, Luqman thought. Do you hear that, Partner? She said Paris!

She talked about the problems and threats that her delegation had encountered during the excavations. She talked about the country's wealth of antiquities, the corruption of the people in charge, and how little they felt responsible. All the while, Luqman was thinking about the type of bomb he would use to nail her heart. A swift and deadly blow that wouldn't require many attempts. There was no time to lose. Just a few short months, and she would leave. Let him be optimistic and say, "Just a few short months, and they would leave."

He had said to her, "If you would show me now what the problem is, Miss Shireen."

She bent over and opened a cupboard in the kitchen to show him cans of food and some bags that had been torn open, their contents scattered everywhere and ruined. He came over and bent down himself to take a look and examine the size and type of droppings the mice had left behind.

She stood up when he did. The pencil fell from atop her head, and her thick, red hair tumbled down around her shoulders and face. A fragrance breathed out and penetrated Luqman's nostrils. He looked at this woman standing so near. Her green eyes shone out from under her glasses, looking at him, embarrassed with the embarrassment of small kids. Luqman tore his eyes away from hers. He tried to make a movement that would make her believe he felt shy and flustered. Then he bent over to pick up the pencil and give it back to her. She thanked him, her face turning red, as she gathered the scattered locks of hair. He left her there and went back into the living room.

She said she didn't want to kill the mice, and that she wanted, if he were able to do it, just to remove them. Oh, the horror! he thought. A woman as small as a mouse who feared mice!

Frowning, Luqman replied, "First, we have to make sure they aren't rats."

He sat at the table after asking for a piece of paper and a pen. He began posing questions to her, as though it were a doctor's examination. She answered, and he recorded her observations until the time came for the diagnosis. He said they were small rats that had visited her by chance, and this meant there was a colony of them that would follow shortly thereafter, as soon as they got the news about the place with abundant food that had been discovered. That's how rats worked. They sent out a scout to reconnoiter, and then the rest follow if the scout stumbles upon any rich game.

Shireen was alarmed. "What's to be done?"

He reassured her. "We'll put out food for them for several days and make it easy for them to get to it. They'll forget their caution and come in large numbers. When they are feeling safe and comfortable, we'll put poison in the food. That way, we'll kill the greatest number of them. When they see all of their dead, they'll become afraid and abandon this spot."

Several weeks. That was the period Luqman would give himself for Shireen to take the bait and fall into his trap. He'd come to see her every day. He'd make her believe he was preparing a special kind of food, which was necessary to renew at least every twenty-four hours. If not, the rats would become disgusted with it, since they love what's fresh and reject anything old. And maybe one day, he'd bring a rat or two along in his bag to release in the apartment so that she'd believe him. That way, his rats would eat her little mouse and create a situation that would have her eating out of his hand.

CHAPTER 11

"Where did I go wrong?"

Lurice tore her eyes from the sky. She walked towards the bedroom of her only son, Elias—or "the Albino." She turned on the light, opened the wardrobe, and began taking out the clothes and piling them on the bed. She came across rolls and scraps of old fabric. She lifted them up, inhaling their scent as mothballs fell out and scattered on the old, decorated tile floor.

Lurice stood motionless, watching them bounce with a profound interest. When the small, white balls had come to rest, she frowned and turned around, trying to remember what she had been doing and what had made her pile up all these clothes. Of course! She had to sew an outfit for her little one. First, she would empty the wardrobe and throw out all these pants, shirts, and suits.

She gathered what she could in her arms and went over to the living-room window. She opened it and began throwing the load into the street. She leaned out to examine what had fallen and smiled while gazing down the narrow street.

She used to stand at that window to see him off with her own two eyes every day as he left for school, and then again to welcome him home. She watched him grow, inch by inch, out of her lap and into the street, his shoulders broadening as he grew taller. She watched his sandals strike the asphalt, waiting for them to wear out just a little so that she could run to the shoemaker. It would not do for her little one to feel any deprivation or to feel different from his friends.

When his father, who had worked as an employee in the electric company, passed away, neither Lurice nor Elias had been sad. They sat together after his departure like a married couple. It was as though the departed was only a temporary guest who had left when it was time to go. The next day, life went on as though nothing had happened, as though things had finally been settled and gone back to normal.

She passed her days sewing, and he would sit across from her, engrossed in his books and notebooks. She would make supper, and they would sit together as he told her what he had done during his long school day. And if he came home and found customers who had come to the house to be measured, he greeted them with a soft voice and, without turning aside, headed immediately to his room until they went out. In this way, Lurice acquired two badges of honor: one for her proficiency as a seamstress and another for her mastery of the principles of child rearing.

Until that accursed day came. That's how she saw it now, though at the time she hadn't noticed anything, nor did she feel that what had happened called for any further attention.

Elias had overslept after staying up late to study. He was nervous because he was taking tests in all his subjects. Lurice had prepared a lunch for him, as usual. She wrapped it in a plastic bag, which she set on the table for him to put in his tote after drinking his glass of milk.

She kissed him, and he went out. She stood at the window to see him off, praying that he would have a clear mind and success on the exams. When he disappeared from sight, she closed the window and sat down at her sewing machine, just as she did every morning.

Lurice finished the dress she was working on. When the clock struck ten-thirty, she got up to go to the kitchen and made herself the cup of coffee she always drank during her morning break. That's when she found it. A plastic bag, with the boy's lunch inside!

Lurice went crazy. What would he eat for lunch? He'd go hungry. Maybe some dizziness would come over him and make him faint. Maybe he would die. Oh, God! She ran to the school after throwing on her overcoat inside out. It was a rainy day. Storm winds blew, and there was thunder and lightning. She arrived and implored the doorman to let her in. Then she implored the principal to permit her be the one to deliver herself what she was carrying.

After a long resistance, the doorman let her in. And after a long pleading and insistence, the principal allowed her to bring the bag to him in his class. She wanted to make certain he got his lunch. She feared the doorman would forget, and after him, the principal. She wanted to catch a glimpse of him, just for a moment, so that she'd be reassured and her heart would stop racing. So that she might see him in his school uniform, like a prince, sitting in the class with the rest of the students.

She knocked lightly on the door. The teacher came and opened it. Lurice leaned her head in to see him. And she did see him. His face went pale. Out of shyness, she thought. He actually was shy. She lifted the bag and waved it at him. He sank in his seat as though he wanted to disappear, as though he were not the one intended by those gestures of hers. He looked down and put his hands over his face. Lurice understood. She wouldn't insist. She whispered his name to the teacher and gave her the bag. Then she left.

When he returned home at the end of the school day, exactly at four-thirty in the afternoon, she got up to go kiss him. He did not greet her, he did not kiss her, and he didn't utter a word. He went directly to his room and locked the door behind him.

She waited. One hour, then two and three, until the clock struck seven-thirty. She knocked, calling him to come out for supper. He didn't answer. She was afraid some accident had befallen him. She implored and called and pleaded until he uttered a single sentence, informing her that he had a lot of homework and studying to do. She didn't say anything. She just put a tray of food on the floor in front of his door and went away.

Elias changed and was never again the same boy. He remained frowning and silent for days. When he did open his mouth, it was to quarrel, fight, complain, curse, and cry. His grades at school got worse.

"In the end, I picked myself up and went to his teacher to ask her if she had any explanation for what had happened to him and made him change like this.

"When I left her, I didn't turn to look at anything. Tears filled my eyes. No! Tears flowed down my face as I talked to myself out loud and sobbed and repeated, 'Lurice, your son is ashamed of you and claims that you are not his mother! She's the maid, he had told them. Yes, the woman who had brought him the bag of sandwiches, me, I wasn't Lurice. Rather, I was the servant his mother sent to bring him the meal. Lurice was one of the society ladies, rich, with an illustrious lineage. Just like the other mothers. The mothers of his friends. How could a seamstress of no account measure up to the kind of society in which Elias lived, the son of the electric company director!

"I didn't tell his teacher he had lied. That he was inventing and pretending and being delusional. I nodded my head and cried while trying to find an excuse that would save him from punishment and allow him to preserve the respect of his instructors. Then I found it. I was the one who had raised him, I told her. I raised him and loved him so much that I sometimes made the mistake of considering him a son.

"And I never informed my little 'master' about my exchange with his teacher.

"And Elias grew up.

"And the war came.

"And things got bad.

"And the roads to his school were closed.

"And he transferred to another school only a quarter-mile from the neighborhood.

"And the boy was different.

"And he started coming home with his friends.

"And I was his mother once again.

"And I forgot.

"And he started going by 'the Albino.'

"And I became the mother of the Albino, the leader of the neighborhood."

The spool of thread on the sewing machine ran out, so Lurice got up to go to the bedroom to look for a replacement. She thought she would go down to the market the next day to stock up on the essentials she had run out of and the various things she needed. She looked at the alarm clock and saw it pointing at exactly a quarter to three. She ought to hurry to get dinner ready. Yes, and there was cake too. When he was hungry, he didn't wait; whenever he waited, he lost his appetite.

She went back to the living room and exchanged the empty spool of thread with a full one. Not bad. The color was close, and the difference wasn't obvious. She finished hemming the shirt quickly and lifted it up. She put it over the pants and stepped back a little to be able to see the two pieces together and check how well they went together.

When he arrived, but before he ate, she would ask him to try them on. This is a gift for you, she would say. And maybe she would add an envelope containing a bit of money for him to buy what he liked. She would kiss him and give him his gifts. She would light the candles and say, "Happy birthday, darling! You are ten years old today!"

The clock in the living room struck three o'clock. Lurice shrieked at it, "Oh my God! One more hour and the school day will be done, and he'll be back!" She hurried to the kitchen.

The big clock kept turning slowly, as it had done for years. And if it had been able to respond, it would have said, "I struck three o'clock, Lurice, it's true. Yet it's not three in the afternoon, as you think, but three in the morning!"

CHAPTER 12

Luqman turned off the printing calculator. He rolled up the long strip of paper and threw it towards Salaam. It streamed out in flight and bounced to a rest on the floor.

Salaam smiled and bent over to pick it up, saying, "Luqman, if you continue your God-awful horsing around, I'll hang this from your neck like a tail. Then I'll make you a fez and label it 'Mr. Devil' in gold letters!"

Days had passed with her in this good mood. It was enough for Luqman to see the bruises on her neck, the cigarette burns on her arms, and the purplish lines on her thighs to understand the reason for her unusual happiness and this light mood of hers. Najeeb, it was God himself who sent you to save me from Salaam and her dreams of marriage.

When he returned that evening from Shireen's place, he had found them eating dinner together. They asked him about the customer, and Luqman tried to put them off with his answer. He concluded by saying they hadn't been able to agree on the price.

Luqman had sat down near them. He took Salaam's head and kissed it, saying, "I didn't mean anything by what I said. By God, you are dearer to me than my sister. You know how bad things are, and the stress and my frayed nerves." He winked at her and added, "Forgive and forget?"

She laughed and nodded, saying, "Of course! Forgiven and forgotten, Luqman."

He discovered the matter of her relationship with Najeeb later on, when he started noticing marks on her face and other traces left behind from the time she spent with Najeeb. At first, she would hide these signs of her newfound love with stylish scarves tied around her neck, with pants, which she seldom used to wear, or with long-sleeve shirts. When Luqman hinted he knew full well what was going on behind his back and that he wasn't opposed, but on the contrary was delighted with how things were turning out between her and Najeeb, she relaxed and began taking pride in displaying the marks she bore, showing them off as badges of honor and decisive proof of her promotion in the ranks of love and relationships.

Salaam started coming to visit nearly every day, and it no longer pained or angered her when Luqman was gone for long hours. Indeed, she matched his absences with further generosity. No matter how badly the business was going, she didn't seem to care about the additional spending money he started asking her for, pleading an unending stream of patently false excuses. In short, Salaam was showering money upon Luqman once again, and he was transformed into something that looked like a businessman.

Meanwhile, Najeeb devoted himself so fully to his experiments that he took on the appearance of a mad scientist. He would open the notebook that Einstein, the man at the institution, had bequeathed to him and spend hours absorbed in reading it. He claimed he was inventing a poison. Not just any poison, but the poison that would wipe out the entire race of rats, every last one of them. The invention would be recorded in his name, and he would take his place among the community of scientists and the rich and famous. He was buying additional books on botany, chemistry, and zoology, and he conducted strange experiments that gave off a mixture of various peculiar odors.

In the end, Luqman's apartment was transformed into what appeared to be a genuine laboratory: test tubes, vials, instruments, and cages filled with rats, mice, and insects that Najeeb hunted in his nighttime rounds of the poor residential neighborhoods and the garbage dumps.

That was when Luqman decided to broach the topic with Salaam. He sought her out one day at work in the telephone exchange.

"Don't you find that Najeeb has been behaving oddly?"

"You mean his experiments and the notebook he's always reading as though it contained all the secrets of the world? What's the problem, Luqman? As long as it distracts him from other women and keeps him in my grasp."

"Sure, but do you see what chaos the apartment has come to? And—"

She agreed with him immediately. "You are so right! We've been a burden on you, Luqman. We've been too much, I know. What if you persuaded Najeeb of the need to move? That way he would have plenty of space to conduct his experiments. He'd be more comfortable, and you could get some rest. Of course, we'd keep your apartment as an office, and—"

Luqman understood. He would suggest to Najeeb that he move to Salaam's house. He wouldn't do it directly. Rather he would make allusions and hint that his apartment was no longer big enough, that he needed some privacy so that he would able to receive the guests he wanted to invite...the female guests he wanted.

"Marina, for example, you old bastard?" Salaam interrupted him, laughing. She added, "Can I count on you? It would be a real service to me, Luqman. I'd never forget it as long as I live, and you'd finally be showing a bit of gratitude to pay me back for all my kindness."

Then, on the day they had settled on, they came together to carry out their plan. And here was Najeeb, coming out of the kitchen with his notebook.

He went over to Salaam and held out the notebook to show her something. "Do you know what this is?" he asked.

Salaam inspected the drawing carefully. She raised her eyes with something that resembled an apology. Najeeb frowned, disappointed, and started to head back in the direction he had come from. Luqman stopped him by asking, "What's the matter?"

Najeeb responded that Einstein had recorded the name of a certain plant in Latin, *Urginea maritima*, but unfortunately, he hadn't come across a translation in the dictionary.

"What does he say about it?" Luqman asked with a wink to Salaam out of the corner of his eye.

Najeeb read aloud, "It's a plant that only grows in the Mediterranean basin. The Greeks, Egyptians, Persians, Arabs, and Romans used it as a diuretic and to cleanse the lungs. The Arabs used it against bedbugs, cockroaches, and the like because it has antimicrobial properties. It varies in height between three and five feet. Its leaves are large and pointy on the ends, and they all grow at the base of the stalk. Its flowers are white or green, which grow in tall bunches from July until September. It has a type of whitish fruit that contains two or three seeds. The root is shaped like an onion and covered in a red rind—"

"Enough!" shouted Luqman, laughing. Najeeb came over and showed him an illustration of the plant torn from a book and pasted onto a blank page in the notebook. "This is the sea onion, man! What's wrong with you, Najeeb? The area around here is full of it. My mother would boil it for us to drink as a remedy for bronchitis, colds, and coughs."

"Hallelujah!" shouted Najeeb, overjoyed. He closed the notebook and sat on the couch next to Salaam, putting his feet up on the coffee table in front of him. He lit a cigarette and took a deep drag, like someone relaxing after a long exertion.

"Whenever something eludes you," Luqman boasted, "you just need to ask Luqman, miracle worker and king of riddles. Any other mysteries troubling you?"

"One or two months at the most, and I'll have the recipe," Najeeb ruminated.

"The recipe? What recipe?" asked Luqman.

"I've solved the problem, Luqman," Najeeb continued. "I was torn between which of two solutions to choose, biological warfare or a chemical extermination."

Luqman laughed. "And what do you intend?"

"Chemical," said Najeeb. "If that doesn't work for me, I'll try the germs."

"Good heavens!" Salaam protested. "And the company? And the accounts I've been going through, where I've discovered losses that threaten us with ruin? What's wrong with you, Luqman? Have you forgotten the goal of our meeting today?"

"The problem is the profusion of rats in the poor neighborhoods and the lack of money in those people's wallets," Najeeb spelled out. "And the solution? We go to some of the rich neighborhoods at night and set some rats free here and there."

"Ingenious!" exclaimed Salaam. "What do you think, Luqman?"

"I have an even better idea," he replied. "We choose a victim, douse him in milk, and set the rats free on him!"

"Luqman! Be serious for once!" Salaam insisted.

But Najeeb concurred enthusiastically. "Of course! We choose a victim and set the rats on him. Then we throw him in a public place where the people will notice and start talking about it. Journalists will come, and the story will be front-page news. You can imagine the fear and the terror, and the calls and the cash…"

"The victim's on me!" Luqman called out.

Salaam laughed. "And who might it be?"

"The doorman!" said Luqman. "My God, how wonderful it would be to see the rats devour him and leave not a trace behind."

"Why shouldn't the lucky lady be the asylum director?" Najeeb countered. "I'd let some purebred rats loose between her thighs to enjoy themselves properly!"

"Or…Marina, Luqman's girlfriend!" proposed Salaam.

"The Communista? Shame on you!" Luqman scolded.

"I don't have anything against her, I swear to God," Salaam protested. "But she's perfect for the job, since who would miss her? She has no family and no friends."

Salaam took advantage of the discussion about women to remind Luqman once more of the goal of their meeting that evening. There was nothing for Luqman to do this time but comply. He set about redirecting the conversation such that all three of them arrived at the same conclusion: that it was necessary for Najeeb to transfer his laboratory to Salaam's apartment, as soon as possible.

CHAPTER 13

"How nice to see you!" the doorman said with a welcoming smile. His eyebrows rose in admiration of Luqman's elegant clothes.

Luqman had become one of the family, and his frequent visits no longer occasioned a call to announce him to Miss Shireen or to confirm that he actually had an appointment with her.

Shireen opened the door for him with a towel in her hand. She brought him into the living room and invited him to take a seat and wait for her to wash her hands—she had been busy cooking, since people were coming over for dinner. Luqman refused to interrupt her work, suggesting he sit with her in the kitchen.

Shireen put the coffee pot on the burner and asked him if he had brought the bill so that she could compensate him for all his labors. He reached into his shirt pocket and brought out a small piece of folded paper, saying, "I hope you won't be surprised at the price."

Shireen read the contents of the paper. She raised her eyes to Luqman and laughed as she shook her head back and forth. "Are you serious? This is too little," she said. "Indeed, you've practically worked for free."

Luqman smiled in turn and said, "All the same, its more than I deserve, Miss Shireen."

She reread the paper and said, "Given that your bill says the price for your labors is that I accept an invitation to dinner, I'm ready to settle things up this instant...on the condition that you be my guest."

Luqman thanked her and said he couldn't stay, given that her friends were from high society and were highly cultured, skilled at languages. "They would inevitably find the presence of someone like me strange—a common man, nearly illiterate, and a rat catcher on top of all that."

Shireen disagreed and said, "I'm very proud to know you."

"Don't feel embarrassed, Miss Shireen. I'll come another time."

"Please, stay."

Luqman was silent. The doorbell rang. Before going to receive the first of her guests, Shireen took him by the hand and decreed, "You'll stay. I need you."

When the guests were gathered around the dinner table, Shireen sat Luqman to her right after introducing him to all of them, and all of them to him. She used the expression, "*mon ami*, Luqman."

They were a mix of nationalities and ages. University

professors, researchers, and archeologists. French, English, Italians, and Germans. Shireen spoke to them all, and from time to time, she leaned over to Luqman and translated for him a summary of what was going on in the conversation.

Until it was his turn. He had been fearing this moment, and here it was, landing heavily upon his chest. One of them turned and said something to him. Luqman remained silent and looked wordlessly at Shireen as though to say, "I warned you!"

She smiled to reassure him. Then she spoke to the man posing the question. All the guests turned to Luqman and examined him with evident interest, as though seeking more information.

Shireen played the role of translator between Luqman and her guests after having informed them of his line of work. One of them jumped in to point out the importance that rat lairs held in the eyes of archeologists, given how they advance the study of the habits and characteristics of a given historical age. That was because the lairs usually contained a large quantity of artifacts and even pieces of money.

Luqman went into detail to display his knowledge on the subject. He was dazzling, sprinkling witty comments in here and there, and in the end, Shireen was mesmerized as she saw the others fall under his spell.

The center of conversation shifted away from Luqman and was divided among several small circles when the guests got up from dining table and went to sit

in the living room. Shireen put on some music and lowered the lights a little. She started picking up glasses and
empty wine bottles to bring into the kitchen.

Luqman stood up and followed, clearing some
ashtrays filled with cigarette butts. She thanked him and
handed him a chilled bottle of champagne. He set it down
on the kitchen table. Then he took her hand and held it
between his own.

Shireen was confused and looked at him with dart-
ing eyes. Was it the effect of the wine she had drunk, or
perhaps was he, Luqman, the cause? To find out, he lifted
her hand to his mouth and kissed it. He kept her fingers
pressed against his lips. Then he looked up and examined
her face, loading his glance with all the yearning in his
heart.

Shireen lowered her head and closed her eyes. No,
he wouldn't kiss her now. He would first take her in his
arms, hold her tight, kiss her forehead, and then let her
go. Shireen was a romantic woman. What she wanted,
first and foremost, was a love story. Sex would come later,
after he had proven to her that he loved her. Silently, tenderly, like a father. Like her father who had passed away.

Luqman went out to the living room with the bottle
of champagne. Shireen went around distributing glasses.
He saw her moving in a different way now, her body suddenly awake as the blood coursing through it colored her
cheeks and animated her limbs.

Shireen took off her shoes and sat on a couch in the
corner. She lifted her hand and undid the knot that tied

her hair. She shook out her hair, and the red, undulating locks exploded, pouring down on her face and shoulders.

She'd take off her glasses after a little, Luqman knew. Indeed, here she was taking them off and setting them down on the floor beside her. She closed her eyes and leaned her head against the wall while squeezing her crossed legs against her chest. What was she dreaming about? Luqman? Perhaps. He'd wait and see.

Someone went over and said something to her. She sat up and answered. She accepted a glass of champagne and took a sip. One small mouthful, then another. She looked towards Luqman. He lowered his eyes to give her the impression that he wasn't looking at her. Rather, to make her think that he meant to give her the impression that he hadn't been looking at her. What do you think, Partner? Don't you see that things always turn out in my favor?

Luqman frowned and strove to project the air of a forlorn lover who saw that intractable and thorny distances came between him and the attainment of his desire. This is what women wanted: a passionate man sending his gaze afar, into empty space, lost in sorrowful passion.

And now she was looking at him again. Her eyes shone with a thousand rays and proclaimed she was a woman who felt as though she were about to enter a love story. All of a sudden, her beauty would combine with the seed a man cast into her heart, making her fall in love at last.

Shireen's guests got up, thanking her and saying

goodbye. Luqman stood, uncertain about what he should do or say. One of the guests, putting his hands on an invisible steering wheel, asked whether he had a car. When Luqman shook his head, the guest offered to give him a ride home.

Shireen, who had been following their discussion out of the corner of her eye, interrupted her own conversation. Turning to Luqman, she breathlessly asked, "Are you leaving too?"

Luqman shrugged his shoulders as though to say, "I don't know."

Shireen went on, "I don't feel tired. You?"

"Me neither," he replied.

She smiled and said, "In that case, let's stay up a little longer."

Luqman went back to the living room and left her to stand with her guests for a few minutes in front of the elevator and say goodbye. He sat on the large sofa and congratulated himself for having taken precautions for this possibility: he had taken a shower, cut his fingernails and toenails, and put on clean underwear, as well as some cologne.

Best not to hurry, Partner: it's a delicate situation. The smallest misstep is liable to lose Miss Shireen, and with her, our Parisian future. You have to get used to this type of woman. Haste doesn't work with them. Take all the time you need. If she means nothing more than staying awake a bit longer, then, I beg of you, keep your head in order to leave her with a good impression—we'll postpone the attack until a future visit, some rendezvous that we might suggest later on.

Shireen closed the door and came back into the living room.

She stood in front of Luqman and looked at him, holding back her emotion.

She hesitated for two or three seconds. Then she threw herself on top of him.

CHAPTER 14

Salaam looked at the director. She could feel her eyes
burning with hatred. Her throat choked with the desire
to go over, kiss her on the mouth, and bite down on her
tongue for as along as it took to shear it off completely.
Then she would throw it on the floor.

Salaam didn't care about anything the director said
about Saleem and about her. She didn't care about the
scolding tone that accompanied her speech, or the long-
winded sermon she poured on Salaam's head like boiling
water. Rather, it was how she talked about Najeeb at the
end and hinted, with a smile full of wicked insinuation, at
what the two of them did together.

It was Salaam's fault. She made things worse, even
though she just meant to respond to the director's fierce
and dastardly attack.

The director had said to her, "Your brother attacked
the psychologist who was treating him for free." (She

emphasized the words "for free.") "Then he ripped open the front of her shirt and threw himself on her, kissing her breasts. When she screamed and tried to push him away, he hit her and began beating his head against the wall, calling out your name."

Salaam said, "I'll apologize and try to make it up to her with a gift."

The director said, "And do you think that's enough? I requested to see you, Miss Salaam, so that you might enlighten me. Perhaps you have an explanation for Saleem's behavior."

Salaam replied, "Wouldn't that be nice! If it were in my power to understand what goes on in his disturbed mind, I wouldn't have resorted to your institution. As you know, Saleem isn't violent. He's like a child. He has a nervous breakdown when someone prevents him from carrying out a desire."

"What type of desires, for example, Miss Salaam?"

Salaam looked at her, surprised at the tone her speech had adopted all of a sudden. A tone that had something of an accusation and some kind of oblique strategy, like the tone of an investigator seeking to extract a confession.

If Salaam failed in this test of strength she sensed was coming, she would certainly lose the entire battle, and Saleem would be the victim along with her. What exactly had this vile director heard? Salaam ought to move her tongue back and forth in her mouth ten times before saying something that would turn out badly.

Salaam took a deep breath, trying to force a smile onto lips that resisted so violently they started to tremble. She said, "How should I know what Saleem wanted when he threw himself on the doctor? She may have been treating him harshly, or asking him to do something he didn't understand. Or else he got a bad vibe about her, or a dark thought came over him. You are putting questions to me that, unfortunately, I have no answers for."

"There's no need for evasion, Miss Salaam. The attendant who watches over Saleem's wing has confessed."

Disturbed, Salaam asked, "And what tales has he been inventing?"

"He didn't invent anything," the director stated. "He swore that during every visit, you would offer him a gift for letting you go in to see Saleem. I did what was necessary and dismissed him from his position at the sanatorium."

"I know direct contact with the patients is forbidden," Salaam allowed. "But who would blame a sister for missing her brother and wanting to be with him and hug him for a while?"

"Just hugging?"

"I don't understand the question."

"What I mean," the director said, "is that the attendant wasn't stupid. He found it strange how the patients would calm down whenever you went in. So he decided to get to the bottom of it."

"What do you mean?" Salaam asked.

"What I mean," the director repeated, "is that the

person in whom you put your trust has betrayed you and revealed your secret. What I mean is that the person you had bribed to let you in to Saleem would make you think he had left, but all the while he was standing nearby to watch what you were doing and how you would act out upon your brother the passion of your longing for him!"

"Lies!" Salaam screamed. "Everything you've said is a lie!"

"You accuse me of lying?" the director challenged. "Me?! You are the liar! For shame! You do forbidden things with your brother, your flesh and blood, your full-blooded sibling, and instead of being ashamed of yourself, you stare me down brazenly. Have you forgotten who you're talking to?"

"No, I've never forgotten that I'm speaking to a respectable lady, who does things so disgraceful one's hair stands on end."

"Get out of my office this instant," the director shouted. "If you don't, I'll expose your secret to everyone!"

"You'll expose me?" Salaam exploded. "I'm the one who will expose you, you whore, you bitch, you shameless slut! I'll tell everyone about all the things you used to do with Najeeb and how you used to force him to do the most outrageous and disgusting things in order to stay out of prison—"

The director could no longer endure Salaam's tirade. She rushed over, slapped her on the face, and dragged her out of the office. There was nothing left for Salaam to do except fight back with every ounce of strength she had. She grabbed the director's hair and twisted her neck back to pull her to the ground. Salaam threw herself upon her and hit, bit, scratched, kicked, and spat until the director's strength was exhausted. She became calm underneath Salaam.

Salaam kept sitting on her as she caught her breath and thought about what she might do with Saleem, now that she had broken the jar and wouldn't be able to put it back together again.

The director opened her eyes and pushed Salaam off. She got up calmly, arranged her clothes and her hair. Then she went to the office and opened the door. She turned to say goodbye with a smile that overflowed with sly malice and dirty insinuation.

That's when she said, "I'm not surprised you rage like a she-devil like this...Najeeb truly is a stallion!"

--

Salaam threw Saleem's things in the trunk. She opened the car's back door and sat him inside. She got in the front and gripped the steering wheel, wrenching it back and forth and almost exploding with rage. She turned the key and set off down the mountain road for home.

What would she do with Saleem now? And what would Najeeb's reaction be when he saw him? She had been expecting everything from the director except that she expel her brother from the sanatorium and force Salaam to take him back. It was all Salaam's fault. If she had kept her mouth shut, it may have been possible to tempt the director with a sum of money. Most likely, that had been the director's plan in sending for Salaam. And if she had stubbornly refused, Salaam would have sent Najeeb to arouse her and pressure her until she agreed.

No! That was something Salaam could not do. That was what she absolutely and positively rejected. It was more than she could possibly endure. Picturing her man between the thighs of another woman was liable to drive her stark raving mad.

She looked at Saleem in the rearview mirror and saw him leaning his head against the window. He wasn't sleeping. No doubt it was the injection of morphine the attendant had given Saleem so that Salaam could bring him out and keep control of him until the two of them got home. She ought to stop by the pharmacy and buy the drugs the doctor had prescribed for him.

If she returned and found Najeeb in the house, how would she explain it to him? How would she justify it? What could she say? And if her brother did live with them, wouldn't Najeeb leave her and disappear just as Luqman was going to do if she hadn't agreed to put Saleem in the asylum?

This question continued to chip away like a chisel at the nerves in Salaam's brain. It became more insistent every time she checked the road and saw the distance that separated her from Najeeb shortening.

What if she played down the matter with Najeeb and just put Saleem in one of the side rooms and locked him up? That way, Najeeb wouldn't have to see Saleem, given that the house was so spacious and the rooms were separated from each other. That wouldn't work at all, she was certain. What's more, who would guarantee the results would be as she wanted? She couldn't take that kind of risk.

Lurice! Why didn't she make Saleem live with her and lock them both up? Of course, this was the ideal solution! She would put them together, and that way, she'd be able to care for them both at the same time, while she lived comfortably in her apartment with Najeeb. And Lurice, would she possibly accept a stranger moving in with her? But what stranger? She knew them both from when they were young, she and her brother, so why would she object? Wasn't it better for her, she who had become an old, senile woman, to live with someone who would ease her loneliness at the end of her life? And Lurice's relative, the guy who came to visit for the morning every Sunday, what would Salaam do about him? How would she justify Saleem's presence and the fact that he was living not in his own apartment with her, his sister, but instead in a different apartment, with a neighbor who was going out of her mind?

Oh, God! What a horrid predicament! What a tragedy had fallen on her head that day! If only you were dead! If only Saleem had died as hundreds of young people had died! She would have been sad, she would have cried for him, her heart would have burst, perhaps, but in the end, she would have forgotten him. All people forget their dead after a time. After a period of mourning, they turn away from them to the preoccupations of life. Then they set aside a small memory in their hearts that makes them cry out from time to time.

As for Salaam, her tragedy, which was named Saleem, was a lamp always set before her eyes. She had gone around with it, walking, breathing, eating, drinking, putting on clothes, expending vast amounts of time and energy and effort, and…and here she was today. Her life would be ruined in the full meaning of the word. In the twinkling of an eye, it would put an end to the honeymoon she had enjoyed with Najeeb, which she thought would go on and transform her life—finally!—from a hell to heaven, from heartache to bliss.

What if she let him out of the car right now and set him free in the street? He would get lost, she would lose all track of him. Then she would cry over him just as so many people had cried over all those who had been kidnapped or gone missing. No, he would return to her—that was certain! Somebody would find him and bring him back to her. Or maybe he would come back on his own without anyone showing him the way.

Five minutes at most, and Salaam would be home. The sweat dripped off her profusely, as though a cloud laden with rain had come to a halt above her head and dumped its load of water all at once. She took her hands off the steering wheel and wiped her palms against her cotton shirt. She ought to stop for a while so she could think clearly. She pulled over to the side of the road, turned off the engine, and looked behind her.

Saleem had closed his eyes. From the rhythm of his breathing she understood he had sunk into a deep sleep. It was just like when he was a little boy and would nod off as soon as he got into a car, or whenever she put him in a cradle and rocked him back and forth to sleep.

CHAPTER 15

Luqman rolled over in bed, luxuriating in the smooth feel of soft sheets on his dark, bare skin. It was the first time Shireen had let him sleep instead of waking him to have breakfast and leave the house together when she went to work.

He lifted his head a little and looked down at his crotch with a smile.

"Good morning, Partner. Well, how did you sleep? I slept like an angel, thanks to you! Yesterday you made your master very happy when he was with Shireen. By my honor, I swear you are my only friend in this world. You are a prince! See how you kept control of yourself and behaved as befits us both. You mastered your reactions until you overwhelmed her senses and made her weep from pleasure and love."

He lifted his eyes and examined the room. He had memorized it like the back of his hand. He had memorized even the clothes, perfume, and other things she kept in her closet, given how long he would sit, watching her get ready after coming out of the shower. He would come to her in the evening after she finished work, and they would spend the night in her bed. Eventually, she had gotten used to his company and could no longer bear his absence, such that she would call if he stayed away for a day or two.

He turned towards the curtain that blocked out the day and guessed from the pale light that filtered through that the sky was still filled with many indecisive clouds. He wanted to open the curtain and look out at the sea, but he didn't have it in him to get up. His glance fell on a piece of paper with a note in Shireen's handwriting. He picked it up and read, "Leave the key with the doorman. If you don't have work, come find me at my site at noon so we can have lunch together."

He looked at his watch and saw that it was eleven o'clock. He ought to get up, take a shower, have some coffee, and then go to her. He shouldn't refuse her invitation to lunch, even if he didn't have any energy or desire to go.

Luqman went into the kitchen, his body and hair still wet from the shower. He walked around barefoot and naked in order to confirm for himself that he was in a familiar place, a place he possessed entirely, a place that didn't make him feel like an intruder or a guest passing through. When a person walks around naked somewhere, he does it for two reasons: either he feels complete ownership and security or…what? Or because the Albino had gotten him!

He remembered the Albino and what he used to do when he subjected his victims to torture. Perhaps it was his small stature and his skinny body that gave him the idea of forcing them to strip off their clothes, take a shower, and remain naked. Certainly, if the Albino had had the body of a stallion like Luqman, then he wouldn't have stripped them in order to enact his barbaric mastery upon them. Most likely, he put them in the bathroom in order to bring them back to the stage of childhood, to make them feel they were children, that he was the man in charge, the voice of complete authority.

How had this not occurred to Luqman before? Perhaps because the Albino used to speak like a prophet who plucked rotten fruit from the baskets of sinners, which he then threw into the fire to be burned in hell. That's what he always used to say. But Luqman perceived now, suddenly, that the Albino's barbarity was just the other side of the coin, hiding his fear, fragility, and feelings of inferiority. Otherwise, what was it that kept him from getting close to women? What made him fall in love with a woman like Salaam?

Luqman opened the cupboard to make his coffee—actually, Nescafé with milk, because Miss Shireen had become afraid that coffee would give him a stomach ulcer or ruin his nerves. He dissolved two sugar cubes in the cup and leaned against the sink, drinking and looking at what was in the pantry.

If she had let him sleep in today and turned the apartment key over to him, it was obviously the first step to him staying at her apartment for successively longer periods of time, until they reached days and maybe even weeks. If she proposed that, he'd resist and, in the end, refuse. It would not do for him to submit to her desires, otherwise they would fade and die over the course of time. If a sense of habit became established between them, he would start feeling familiar to her. And if he felt familiar, the stability in their relationship would displace the blaze of emotions that led her to make decisions that had no basis in deliberation and rational thinking. If Shireen actually reflected and thought about what she was doing, she'd become conscious of the enormous chasm that separated them, and she would realize she needed to break things off some day.

Luqman wouldn't leave her alone to arrive at such a conclusion. He would continue to pursue the line he had followed with her from the beginning. Instead of watching and waiting, he would seize the initiative and attack. He would bring her fears and wonderings into the light so that they would appear outside of herself, as though they were inside him instead. That way, like the fiercest enemy, she herself would strive to fight them, rout them, and destroy them. That's how he made her ask him to stay for dinner the first time. And that's how he would push her to get rid of everything that held her back. She would drop, fully ripened, into the cauldron of his desire, entrusting herself to him completely.

--

Luqman stood on the Corniche and looked up and down the street, hoping a taxi would come soon. He knew he'd be late for lunch with Shireen.

Luqman shouted to an empty taxi, and it braked. He got in and informed the driver of the address. The driver was delighted at this unexpected fare. Then, to show his good mood, he asked Luqman, "Did the tremor wake you up last night, sir?"

"What tremor? When? Where? How?"

The driver explained, "The world is turned upside down, and it's the talk of the town! At about two o'clock last night, my wife and I woke up, and the bed was shaking us as though someone had grabbed it and was jerking it back and forth with all his strength. The kids woke up too and were screaming in terror because the walls had begun to shake so much we imagined they would burst and fall in upon us..."

Luqman thought he hadn't noticed any of this because he was in bed on top of Shireen. And maybe the firm foundations of the building had reduced the effect of the earthquake, such that none of the neighbors had felt it.

The driver continued. "After years of war, misery, the economic crisis, the chemical waste they dump into the sea, the rotten food they distribute in the markets, the last thing we needed to experience it all was an earthquake. This is the wrath of the Lord. The Lord does not strike you with a stone, but he tries his servants by indirect means, so they might repent and seek his help."

The driver stopped for a passenger shouting out his destination and gestured for him to get in the back. After a few more yards, he did the same thing for another passenger flagging him down.

Luqman looked at the driver, astonished at this insolence of his. How is it that you take other passengers, he thought, when I've hired you as a taxi and reserved the entire car? But he checked his words, remembering that he was late and that he didn't have the energy to initiate a quarrel.

The driver turned on the tape player. A singer's voice boomed out, together with a noisy confusion that Luqman knew must be a wedding reception or something like that. There were children squealing, shouts of encouragement, and rapturous praise.

Proudly, the driver announced, "This is the voice of my nephew, and the party here is his wedding reception. He's been trying to become a singer for so long. He even attempted suicide one night because his father refused that career."

One of the passengers in the back interjected, "Your nephew has an excellent voice. But if you turned it down a bit, it would be much better."

Luqman thanked the passenger silently and turned to look at him. He made a bet with himself that this passenger was one of those university students who only listened to rock music.

The driver gave a long blast on the car horn, which he accompanied with a stream of curses, abuse, gestures, and spit as the car joined a long and snarled traffic jam.

A Sri Lankan housekeeper bent over and asked the driver if he was headed to a certain area. He asked her if she was going to pay the fare for an entire taxi. She shook her head, saying she would pay the fare for one seat, no more, no less. The driver exploded in her face, saying he wouldn't take customers like her in his car and advising her to look for a helicopter if she wanted to reach that distant destination of hers within a week. He ended by saying that the Sri Lankans were behaving not as servants but as masters, and woe to him who fell into the clutches of a black slave, for arrogance was the hallmark of the damned blacks.

Luqman saw he had been right about that passenger in the back when the young man commented, "This is racism, uncle!"

The "uncle" turned on him instantly, sparks flashing from his eyes, and growled, "Uncle? May God strike you blind! Out of my car now!"

The young man got out, and the driver slammed the door shut behind him. The driver railed on, "Kids these days! By God, it's like a turd coming from my ass to lecture me."

After the car had been stuck in traffic for quite a while, Luqman peeled his back, wet with sweat, off the leather of the front seat. Perhaps a little air would get in there. If this weather continued, he thought, with the blazing heat and glowering clouds, it was liable to cause an enormous earthquake. He lifted a hand to shield his ear from the sun, which had been pouring heat on his head ever since he left the house and got into the taxi.

It occurred to him to get out and continue on his way by foot. But calculating the distance left, he saw it was still a long way off, much further than he had already gone in the taxi. He would wait a little longer. If the traffic continued to be frozen solid, he'd get out and go directly home. Then he would call Shireen and explain what had happened.

He didn't know how she saw him, but the woman came running from far away, calling his name and waving to him. She leaned through the car window to give him a kiss. Given that the traffic still wasn't going anywhere— moving with the speed of a tortoise, if at all—Luqman opened the door and got out to greet her.

"Marina! What a happy surprise! Since when do you get up so early in the morning to walk the streets?"

By means of a peculiar language consisting of many pantomimed gestures and a few Arabic words she had mastered in the months she had been there, Luqman understood that she had left some time ago the nightclub where she had been working, and that she was engaged or married, and Luqman could no longer understand when she began jabbering in English without pausing to take a breath.

The second passenger in the back, who was sitting by the window, offered, "She's telling you she got engaged to a guy from the countryside and that she's about to travel with him there to perform the civil marriage ceremony and then go on a honeymoon."

Luqman turned towards him and found the man looking at Marina with a smile, encouraging her to go on after having autonomously appointed himself intermediary.

"Where are you traveling?" the passenger asked her. She replied, and he translated for Luqman. "She is going to Europe, and her first stop will be Paris."

Luqman laughed. "Paris all at once, Marina? My goodness!"

The passenger continued speaking English with Marina. Then he directed his words to Luqman. "She says he works as a businessman, that his financial situation is excellent, and that he is young and good-looking."

Luqman looked at the passenger. He knit his brows as if to say, "What place is it of yours to interfere and pose questions on your own accord?" But when his tongue moved, different words came out of his mouth: "Thanks for your help. We've imposed on you."

The passenger didn't take the hint. Instead, he opened the door and got out of the car to stand with them and continue talking to Marina. She had begun responding to him, believing him to be one of Luqman's friends.

Luqman looked at him, not believing his eyes. He got close and put his hand on the man's chest, giving him a little push. "I thanked you, and our business together was done. What's your problem that you keep butting in?"

"I'm talking to her, not you!" the passenger responded. Then he said something in English that made Marina burst out laughing while looking at Luqman and shaking her head.

The blood rushed to Luqman's face when he saw the man mocking him. He grabbed his shoulders, shoved him against the car, and began throwing punches at his head.

The driver honked for them to get in because the traffic was stirring and the cars in front were moving away. Meanwhile, those behind began blasting their horns to urge them forward. There was nothing for the driver to do but get out himself and yell, "If you want to fight, do it, but not on my dime. Pay first, and then kill each other if you want to!"

The street became packed again as people gathered around Luqman and the passenger, trying to separate them. Meanwhile, Marina, who had finally understood what was going on, was yelling and hitting the passenger in the head with her purse.

Pedestrians passing by got between them. They pushed Luqman into the car and gave the driver the fare they took from the bloodied passenger. The driver drove off quickly as people pounded on the roof of the car to speed him on his way.

--

From a distance, Luqman saw her standing in a group of young people. He noticed they were all dressed in jeans and wearing hats. What was this strange profession that forced people to dig up the ground under the burning sun in the middle of this immense quantity of dust? And why? To bring out rocks, bones, shards of pottery, and utensils eaten away by rust and dirt. Dear Lord, sometimes you just didn't know what makes people tick!

Luqman greeted Shireen and saw she was frowning, which was unlike her. He thought she was mad because he was late, but as soon as he opened his mouth to explain what happened, she interrupted him, apologizing for not being able to go to lunch with him because something had come up that she and her colleagues had to discuss. He told her he wasn't in a hurry and that he had plenty of time to wait for her. She shook her head irritably and went back to join the debate.

A young man was saying, "They've exploited the anxiety of the people and the media over the earthquake to send in excavators and bulldozers."

A girl agreed, "It's not enough for them to uproot foundations from the Hellenic period and the walls of the Roman baths, but they parked their equipment on top of the site we discovered a few days ago, where the Phoenician cemetery extends!"

"I'll call the people in charge," declared Shireen.

The young man looked at her in disbelief. "What's wrong with you, Miss Shireen? Who do you think sent the excavators and gave the orders to bulldoze it all?"

"What about the newspapers?" Shireen asked.

A man wearing glasses explained, "It was because of

the campaign waged by the press that the officials promised publicly in the newspapers and magazines, to allow a process of taking everything apart for numbering and photographing. That way, the stones could be transported and reassembled. And the result? They just bulldozed it all, even before we were able to number a single stone!"

The young man: "What do they care about antiquities? What concern is it of theirs if something thousands of years old is destroyed? What's necessary is to finish the reconstruction of the city's commercial center so money can be invested and profits returned to them as soon as possible."

The girl: "After excavations revealed the city was founded approximately five thousand BC, after preliminary drilling discovered eighty thousand square meters of archaeological sites revealing successive layers of civilizations—Canaanite, Phoenician, Hellenic, Byzantine, Roman, Mamluk, and Ottoman—Parliament and the Ministry of Culture signed an agreement with UNESCO establishing the need to protect all these antiquities. But it was only a matter of weeks before Parliament itself, without batting an eyelash, issued an order to fill in one of the most important excavations. They covered over unique ruins and entire Roman columns in order to replace them with flowers and a clock tower."

The young man: "Or don't you know, Miss Shireen, about what one of the officials said in response to a journalist's question: 'We'll bury the antiquities in sand and plastic bags in order to preserve them, and we'll plant flowers in their place to project a civilized appearance.' A civilized appearance! And regarding the fate of the agreement made with UNESCO, he replied, 'The project costs money, and we don't want to pay. The world is on one path, and you are on another. The country is in a squalid condition, and we all have to tighten our belts.'"

The man with the glasses: "And the archeological site they filled just to make a parking lot? And—"

The girl: "Of course, they talk about a squalid condition as long as it's connected to a project that's in the interest of the country! As for the scandal of theft, plundering, and embezzlement on the part of government officials, there's no talk of squalor and account books."

The young man: "We're finished! What good does talking do? What do you all expect from a country that doesn't respect its history—"

The girl: "Rather, a country that has lost its memory to the point of having no roots at all! Enough! I'm sick of it! Wouldn't it have been better for me to have majored in something other than archeology?"

The young man: "Business, for example, or the service industry..."

The group broke up. They went their separate ways with heads bowed and feet dragging like a vanquished army unit.

Shireen turned to Luqman. She looked at him with dejection. "Tell me, what is it that made my father conceive me here, and what did I come looking for in this country?"

CHAPTER 16

Salaam was uneasy when she reached the front of the line and someone was standing behind her, waiting for his turn after hers. She had wanted to be alone in order to take her time as she spoke. But the pharmacist was staring at her with dwindling patience, so she asked him for a gauze bandage, which she paid for and left.

Where would she come across an empty pharmacy, without any other customers? A pharmacy with an agreeable owner, who wouldn't ask too many questions, and who didn't live near her neighborhood, such that it would be unlikely for her to run into him?

Salaam started the car and took a quick look at the time. It wouldn't do for her to be late. Saleem hadn't eaten dinner yet, and Najeeb would be home before long.

She remembered an old pharmacist on the other side of the city, whom she had used to go to because he had remained open during the war, even though his pharmacy was situated right on the front lines. She used to go there because his supplies rarely ran out, and Lurice needed an enormous quantity of sleeping pills and sedatives.

He was standing behind the cash register, staring through his thick glasses at medicine bottles and punching in their prices with his gnarled, trembling fingers. Salaam took a deep breath. Now he was speaking to a customer who appeared to be about to leave. She went in and greeted them. Then she stood, waiting for him to finish his conversation.

"Xanax isn't a sleeping pill," the pharmacist insisted. "It's a drug for anxiety and panic attacks. It has harmful side effects if you continue taking it a long time, or if you stop all at once."

"But it relaxed me more than Prozac did," objected the customer. "And my neighbor has been taking it for years, and it hasn't hurt her at all, just the opposite—"

Irritated, the pharmacist interrupted her. "Are you going to teach me my profession, ma'am? Then you can take your business elsewhere. I don't sell medication that constitutes a health risk...I gave you ten milligram tablets of Tranxene, which calms the nerves and helps for sleeping too. Come back with a prescription from your doctor, and I'll give you Xanax, Prozac, and even poison if you want to kill yourself!"

The customer threw the bag of medication she had bought a moment earlier. "Give me my money back!" she yelled. "I don't want this anymore!"

The pharmacist gave her the money back, and she

went on to say as she was heading for the door, "In any case, what's it to you, mister? Are you my brother, my father, my husband, or my nephew that you fear for my health more than I do myself? I'm free to take whatever medicine I want! Shouldn't you have just said from the beginning that you didn't want to sell?"

The pharmacist took off his thick glasses. He took a handkerchief out of his pocket and wiped his forehead and his moist eyes. He put his glasses back on and took a deep breath to suppress his exasperation. Then he turned to Salaam and asked her what she needed.

Salaam smiled and thought about how she might comment on what had just happened in front of her. She was hoping to win some additional time to find how best to broach her subject. So she said, "Everybody these days is suffering from a nervous disorder."

The old pharmacist shook his head as if to say, "It would be better to avoid talking about it." Then he repeated his question a second time. "Excuse me, but you didn't tell me what you were looking for."

"It seems you don't recognize me, Mr. Tawfiq. I'm Salaam. I came here so many times during the war to buy medicine for Mrs. Lurice. Don't you remember?"

The pharmacist hit his forehead with his hand. "Of course! Forgive me! It's no doubt my age and the cataracts in my eye. I've truly become senile, and my memory has started playing tricks on me."

"And why shouldn't you hand over the work to your children and have a rest? Haven't you exerted yourself enough?"

"My children?" replied the pharmacist dismissively. "God forbid! They have all left the country. At first, I was angry with them for leaving me alone when I was an old man. Today, every time one of them calls me, I convince him that he needs to stay where he is and not look back... In any case, how are you, and how is the health of Mrs. Lurice?"

"I'm fine, praise God. But Lurice..."

Salaam's voice trembled and then fell abruptly silent as a lump got caught in her throat and prevented her from continuing.

The pharmacist hurried to bring her a cup of water. He sat her on a chair and tried to calm her down, using traditional phrases about being patient and arming one-self with faith. When Salaam appeared to have calmed down, the pharmacist asked her to tell him what was wrong: she'd feel a release from her grief, and he might see if there was anything he could do to extend a helping hand.

"I swear to God, Lurice is like my mother. But I can't take it anymore," Salaam confessed.

"Does she still suffer from the loss of her son after all these years?"

"If only! But just when she began to forget her loss and regain a capacity for living, she started to complain about bouts of atrocious pain in her head. There wasn't a doctor I didn't bring her to. There was nothing I didn't try for her, and you know, Mr. Tawfiq, the hassle of dealing with doctors and the costs of appointments, medication, and hospitals these days. The important thing is that they discovered she had a malignant tumor in her brain. We had an operation done on her, after which she lost her vision. But the bouts of pain keep coming back and leave her bedridden."

The pharmacist sighed. "There is no power and no strength except with God. But look, he has deprived her of her son and her eyesight, yet he has provided her with a most respectable daughter. May God reward you, Mrs. Salaam! For people like you—humane, honorable, and merciful—have become a rare coin these days. Well, just tell me what I can do to help with this heavy burden."

A swindler's flash glittered in Salaam's eyes. "Every time Lurice needs a shot of morphine to ease her pain, I have to go to the doctor for him to write me a new prescription. And every time, he makes me pay the entire bill for a checkup."

"Morals have gone to hell when doctors become businessmen!" the pharmacist averred.

"So here I am. I've left her at home alone, crying out in her pain. I told myself I'd come find you, and maybe your heart would feel pity, and you would give me the morphine without a doctor's prescription."

The pharmacist was silent, thinking. Then he looked at Salaam, uncertain as to how to answer.

There was nothing for Salaam to do but stand up and say, "It's okay. I see you are in a difficult position, and I know that you are an upstanding man who doesn't like to play around with the law. Forgive me, I've taken up too much of your time, and I ought to go home now. If I'm late, I'm afraid there'll be an accident and something bad will happen to Lurice."

The old pharmacist didn't let her leave. With the beads of sweat dripping off him, he decided to sell her what she came for. Indeed, he added an open invitation for her to come back whenever she needed more.

Salaam paid for the morphine, needles, tape, and disinfectant she needed. Then she left, thanking the pharmacist and praying for his health and long life.

CHAPTER 17

Salaam tucked the pharmacy bag under her arm and picked up the tray of food. She slowly went down the five small steps that separated the front door from the basement. She set the tray on the ground, took the key out of her pocket, and opened the door.

Just like it always did, the smell of dampness and mold surprised her. She closed the door behind her and remained fixed in place, waiting for her eyes to adjust a little to the pitch blackness before feeling her way to the candle amid the boxes and other things piled everywhere.

May you rest in peace, Albino! Here you were, stealing all this stuff and storing it up, yet you didn't benefit from it at all when you departed this life. Why didn't Salaam sell it for a pretty penny? Lurice would go crazy. Salaam hadn't even dared ask her for the key to the basement after bringing Saleem home from the asylum. She just kept searching for hours until she found it. She got lucky and came across it by chance, hidden under Lurice's pillow. If she hadn't, she would have been forced to bring her brother to live in the house, and Najeeb would have figured out by now what was going on.

Salaam lit a match, but it went out. She lit another, and the candle's wick took the flame and began to dance, casting strange shadows on the walls. She went over to Saleem and found him with his eyes open, lying on a blanket on the floor. She peeled the tape off his mouth, taking care not to hurt him, and he lifted his hands to indicate that she untie the rope that bound his hands and feet.

Salaam undid Saleem's bonds. Then she began rubbing the rope marks on his wrists and ankles so that the blood would circulate. After sitting him up and leaning his back against the wall, she lifted the tray onto his lap for him to eat. Saleem put the tray back on the floor. Frowning and with brows knit, he stared at the floor with a pout.

Salaam sank the spoon into the bowl. She lifted the spoon to push it into his mouth, but he swung his hand up to knock it away. The spoon's contents fell onto Salaam's shirt. Saleem looked at her, afraid she would punish him with a blow, but she didn't. Instead, she just put the tray aside and lay down on the ground next to him.

Saleem stretched out beside her. He began licking the food that had landed on her chest. Salaam closed her eyes and let him pull away the fabric that came between him and her breast. She would let him do that for a while. Then she would reach her hand slowly to the bag, take out a needle of morphine, and inject it into his arm. That way, he would sleep soundly all night. She would tie him up again, lest he wake up too early or make some noise, alerting Najeeb that he was down in the basement.

It was good the pharmacist had believed her ruse and had given her what she requested, with a promise to supply everything she needed later on. Otherwise, how could she have controlled Saleem? And how could she have kept people from discovering her secret, that he was living with her? Here she was, feeding him, washing him, and taking care of him. As long as she kept him on morphine, it didn't hurt him to live in the dark or to be gagged, with hands and feet tied. He just slept all the time, not feeling a thing.

She ought not be gone much longer. She had told Najeeb she was bringing dinner to Lurice and would stay with her for a little before coming back to him. She had left Najeeb in the laboratory, surrounded by his plants and his rats, and went out slowly, aware he wasn't paying any attention to what she said. He didn't snap out of it and talk to her except when he was hungry. He would call her, she would prepare food, and they would eat. Then he would leave her alone for another hour or two until he got tired, when he would come into her bed to requite her for taking care of him and letting him work in peace.

She didn't notice Saleem until he had gotten on top of her. She shook him off, alarmed at how her distraction had allowed him to do what she had been forbidding for the past two weeks. He got back on top of her and pinned her arms to the ground. Salaam tried to squirm out from under him, but he fought to hold her and cried out. She feared to resist any further, lest his yelling expose her secret to Najeeb, so she put a hand on his mouth and smiled at him. Then she drew his head down to her shoulder, caressing his back and his shoulders. She stretched out her arm, feeling for the pharmacy bag. She put her hand inside and slowly drew out the needle. Then she brought it up and jammed it hard into Saleem's shoulder.

--

Salaam found Najeeb waiting in the living room, which was unusual for him. She apologized for being late and said she had been worried about Lurice, who was becoming a child again in her fear of being left alone in the dark. Salaam went into the kitchen after letting Najeeb know it wouldn't take her long to get dinner ready.

Najeeb called to her, "I'm not hungry."

Salaam looked at him, finding it strange that his voice was so weak and his face damp with sweat. She asked if he was tired. He didn't answer but just headed off to the bedroom, dragging his feet.

"Wake me in an hour," he told her. "I'm going to lie down for a while to rest."

Salaam started going around the house to take care of some chores. She moved some furniture to sweep, and when she had finished, she dusted. Next, she brought a bucket of water and began to mop.

Her slippers were bothering her, so she took them off and walked around barefoot. Some of the cold from the floor tiles transferred into her body, and she stopped for a moment, pressing on her kidneys with both hands. She listened intently to make sure that a noise she heard wasn't coming from the basement. Then she made fun of herself about how much she worried.

By this time, Saleem would be soaring in the seventh heaven. She had jammed the needle into his shoulder and squeezed the plunger. When Salaam had pushed him off of her and saw she had emptied the syringe entirely, she was afraid she had given him too much morphine because Saleem was seized by a fit of convulsions and started writhing about and knocking his head against the floor. But he became quiet again, and Salaam approached to put her ear to his chest. When she was reassured that his heart was still beating, she got up, blew out the candle, and left him.

His violent attack had surprised her, making her frightened and agitated when she injected him. Some time ago, he had stopped being satisfied to suck her breasts, and he had tried to do other things that made her hair stand on end. She wondered where he had learned such things, forgetting that he had become a full-grown man, lacking nothing except a sound mind. How should she respond in the future?

The best thing would be to keep him tied up and feed him with her own hand, and...and what if he began crying out, and Najeeb heard? That shouldn't be a problem. She would inject him first with morphine, and when he went limp and his eyes started rolling in their sockets, she would remove his gag. Then she would feed him, change his clothes, wash him, and leave him there. She would no longer give him her breast. What were these wicked things that he began asking her for as though they were proper?

Saleem had gone to sleep without dinner. She would go down early the next morning, or if Najeeb was still asleep, she would steal out that night to go down and make sure that he was okay.

Salaam finished mopping and stood in the corner. She opened the front door and began waving it back and forth in the hopes of bringing an additional gust of air to speed the drying process. She thought about waking Najeeb, but she changed her mind when she remembered the strain and fatigue etched into his features. She would let him sleep for a while longer. If he woke up on his own while waiting for her to finish cleaning the bathroom and the kitchen, he would have gotten an extra half hour. And if he didn't, she'd go herself to wake him.

She passed near the room that Najeeb had transformed into a laboratory. She thought about going in to see what had become of it, but she decided against it when she remembered the fear that seized her upon seeing the rats, even if they were securely imprisoned in their cages. How long would he persist in this madness, she wondered. She took strength by telling herself that this madness of his certainly was what kept him with her.

When would Najeeb notice her and open a conversation about his love? When would he ask her to get married? It's true that he had lived with her for weeks. It's true that he never neglected her. And it's true that he slept in her bed, slept with her, and provided for her desires better than any husband. Nevertheless, Salaam needed the title, the description, the name.

"Mrs. Salaam? She's the wife of Mr. Najeeb!"

She longed to hear people utter this sentence just once in her life, and then let her die afterward, it didn't matter! She would talk to Luqman about it. A long time had passed since she last saw him. God alone knew what had happened to him and to the affairs of the business. Tomorrow she would call him, and maybe invite him to dinner. Before everything else, she'd commission him to press Najeeb on the subject of marriage. Let Luqman ask him sometime when they were alone, as though she didn't know anything about the matter. That way, she'd see whether the idea of matrimony with her was appealing to him, or at least, whether she was appealing to him.

Salaam turned off the faucet and shook the water from her hands. She was too tired now to wipe down everything she had washed. She'd let it evaporate slowly and wouldn't make herself use a towel to dry everything. She felt hunger biting her stomach. She looked at the clock and saw that it was exactly ten. What should she do? Should she wake Najeeb now that he had spent more than two hours fast asleep?

Salaam headed for the bedroom and opened the door slowly. She went over to Najeeb on her tiptoes. He was still sleeping. She wasn't able to make out his expression because of the dark, but she heard the sound of his deep snoring. She got undressed and took out her nightgown. She wouldn't wake him. She would have supper by herself, and then she would go to sleep too. It wouldn't hurt her to go to bed early for once, even if she was choking on her desire for him.

Salaam swallowed a last mouthful from her bowl and got up to put the leftovers back in the refrigerator. She heard Lurice's footsteps overhead. She listened carefully and tried to discern what the unhinged old woman was doing at this late hour of the night. Salaam had been neglecting Lurice ever since Najeeb came to live with her. Salaam no longer had the time to cook for her and look after her like before. She began bringing Lurice bags of groceries and letting her manage things on her own. Often, Salaam forgot to look in on her, or pretended to forget, in order to avoid Lurice asking her to do the things she couldn't do on her own. How many hands did Salaam have to look after everyone? Wasn't her work in the Central and the house enough for her, together with taking care of Najeeb and Saleem?

Saleem...She wouldn't feel at ease and certainly couldn't fall asleep as long as he had gone to sleep without supper. He hadn't eaten a thing all day, so how could she leave him like that, hungry and tied up, like an animal? She would go down and try to wake him. Then she'd shove something into his mouth so she could relax.

--

Salaam stood up and pushed her fingers into her eyes to see if maybe they would grant her a few tears. She rubbed them a second time and waited. Nothing.

It was the first tear that resisted her. She renewed her request. One tear, just one, and then the water poured down until her shirt was dripping on the floor. But it was sweat that flowed. A monotonous sound began ringing in her head: a single sentence, the meaning of which she soon lost as it began to circle in the void.

Saleem was in the same position she had left him, stretched out on the blanket, the only difference being a thread of saliva that ran from the corner of his mouth, down his cheek, chin, and neck to puddle on the floor.

She had moved him a little, but he didn't stir. She shook him, and he felt even more rigid. Finally, she understood. She moved away, begging for the tears.

He was dead. Just like those who were murdered, even if there was no premeditation or intent. By a needle of morphine, a massacre, or a sniper's bullet. This is what was repeating in Salaam's head while she stared at him as though looking into the face of a stranger.

She looked at his tied hands and thought the length of his fingernails looked strange. She came closer and untied his bonds. Then she stretched out on the floor. She took the flaming candle and set it next to him. She lifted his hand to her mouth and started biting. She kept biting and spitting until she had chewed down the nails on all ten fingers. And when she was satisfied about the clean appearance of his hands, she folded his arms across his chest. She wiped the spittle away from the corner of his mouth with her hand. She positioned the head in line with the body. She ran her fingers through his hair to arrange the locks that had gotten long and hung down in his face. Then she stared at him again.

Wouldn't it have been better if her features had shared the beauty and symmetry of Saleem's? Wouldn't it have been better if he had come in her place? If she had been the boy, and he the girl? This is what they—family, relatives, and neighbors—used to say in front of them both when they were children. How right they were! If Saleem had been the girl, he and the Albino would have been the same age, and the Albino would have loved him. And if Salaam had been a boy, she wouldn't have been afraid of the war or felt cowardice. She would have become the leader of the neighborhood. Saleem wouldn't have gone crazy, and she wouldn't have been described as an ugly spinster. If only...

Salaam put her hand on her breast and pinched down hard. She didn't feel any pain. Indeed, she didn't feel anything. Not exactly: she felt annoyed. A great annoyance, and an overpowering desire to sleep. Drowsiness began to rise in her like water rising over her and inundating all sensation inside her. What if she stretched out here, next to him, put her arm under her head, and went to sleep? If she did that, she would doze off immediately, in a second or less. She would sleep comfortably and deeply, as though relieved of a heavy burden she had shouldered for years. She would sleep, without needing the sleeping pills she resorted to like a lighthouse guiding sleep to her eyes. She would sleep. Just sleep. As people do. Just as sleep was meant to be. Like a cow dozing off in a safe pen. As though everything that had happened hadn't happened.

As though all of creation would begin afresh tomorrow...

Salaam fell asleep.

She didn't know if it was for minutes or for hours. But when she woke up, she felt energy steal through her limbs as at the start of a new day. She stood up and brushed the dust off her nightgown. If she hadn't stopped to think about the work that was in front of her, she would have forgotten why she was in the basement at that moment.

She went up the five steps and entered the house, heading immediately for the room she had started to call Najeeb's laboratory. She opened the door as though she weren't about to do what would have terrified her merely to think about a day ago. She bent over and grasped a metal handle. Then, with a solid movement, she lifted the cage without paying the least attention to what began scurrying and squealing inside it.

She went down the five steps and set the cage down on the threshold. Opening the door, she went over and blew out the candle. She turned around to go back out. Her foot collided with something warm and supple. She crushed it as though stepping on a sponge that had the feel of meat. She nearly fell over, but she reached out and caught onto something. In maintaining her footing, she knocked over some boxes as well as various other things that began crashing down and rolling around with a clatter.

That didn't phase her. She took the cage and turned it to face the basement. She raised the small latch that closed the cage and gave it a kick with her foot. The rats shot out quickly, running together all over the basement floor.

Salaam put the lock back in its place on the basement

door and closed it. It gave a solid click, confirming that it was secure. She listened intently, and sounds reached her ear that resembled the noise of an iron tool scratching a glass surface, a blade chopping flesh, a saw catching on a wooden object before tearing it up.

Reassured as to what was going on, she decided to go up and lie down to sleep. She carried the empty cage and went up the five steps. Before entering the house, she turned to the sky and saw it was just as it had been, full of clouds. Tomorrow, she would forget. Tomorrow, there would be no trace of the secret that had been hidden in the basement. At that moment, the rats were gathered around him, jumping on him, biting, gnawing, tearing, and eating until they obliterated him completely, as though he had not been here, or as though he had never existed at all.

Salaam opened the door of the apartment, went inside, and closed it behind her.

She went up to the bed and lay down beside Najeeb. She opened her eyes and she rolled over onto her right side, looking for a comfortable sleeping position. When she found it, she closed her eyes and settled into a smile.

Now Saleem was returning to the bosom of his parents in order to return the favor.

He died, first of all, to thank her.

Second, he died to liberate her.

And third, he died to absolve her.

He died and made the rats eat his corpse. He was leaving in order to make sure that no one would bother his sister, pursue her, or accuse her of committing any crime at all.

CHAPTER 18

Shireen called, asking if he could come over as soon as possible.

"Of course," he answered. He left the apartment immediately and went to her.

He found Shireen dressed in a nightgown. Her eyes were tired, and so was she. It was unusual for her to be at home at this time of the day.

"Are you sick?" he asked. She didn't answer and ran instead to the telephone, which had begun to ring.

Luqman went in to the living room and took a seat. When he saw she was engrossed in a conversation that might take a while, he picked up a newspaper lying nearby and began flipping through its pages.

Wasn't this the gleaming, snow-white Marina? What was she doing in the photo, and why were so many policemen surrounding her?

"A Russian prostitute was arrested in possession of

five kilograms of heroin..."

The Communista? Really?

Luqman's eyes began jumping back and forth between the photo and the small black print. He wasn't able to connect the person discussed in the article with that girl in the photo, who looked as frightened as a child who had lost her parents in the airport.

"...The goods were found packed into twenty wooden clothes hangers...The woman, who has been identified as Marina Ostropovich, was headed for Paris to meet her fiancé, who had gone there ahead of her. He is one of the most important drug dealers and has been identified as..."

Shireen finished her conversation and came to sit near him. Luqman folded the newspaper and set it aside in order to take her in his arms and press her head against his shoulder. This way, she wouldn't notice the shock imprinted on his face from seeing the photos and commentary in the newspaper. He stroked Shireen's hair as he recalled his last meeting with Marina. She had been perspiring happiness when she told him she was leaving for Paris.

After a few moments, Shireen sat up and turned to him. She said, "Luqman, I've resigned from my job."

"Is that what has made you so unhappy? You scared me! I thought there had been some catastrophe."

Shireen was silent, frowning. She went on, "There's something else I have to tell you. I've decided to go back to Paris."

"Paris!" Luqman cried out. "When?"

Shireen said, "As soon as I finish some necessary matters. As soon as possible."

Luqman was shocked. He stared at the floor. This truly was a catastrophe! What could he do now? What should he say to her? She had already settled the matter and taken her decision without the least thought to his existence.

Luqman stood up and put his hands in his pockets. He walked over to the balcony. And now what do you suggest, Partner? Any advice? Do you see what has happened? You were so proud of yourself. You claimed to have taken firm hold of the reins, thinking she was hooked on you and would never be able to leave. Yet here she is, bidding you farewell, not taking you into consideration at all. It won't hurt her a bit to be separated from you. I sincerely congratulate you!

Shireen followed him out onto the balcony. She stood near him and raised her hand to stroke his back tenderly. Luqman turned to her with brows knit. Then he took a chair and sat down. She took one too and sat facing him.

"There's nothing more beautiful than the Mediterranean," Luqman said, as he stared into the sea. "From now on, I'll think about it differently, and I'll love it more, knowing you are on the opposite shore."

Shireen swallowed hard. She put her hand to her neck as though to massage the lump that was caught in her throat. The telephone rang. Luqman smiled. He looked at her and nodded. She didn't move from her seat, and the ringing stopped.

"Do you know what?" Shireen ventured. "I only accepted this position and came here in order to forget an impossible love story. Now look at me! I've fallen into one that's much more complicated."

"And you haven't forgotten yet—is that why you have decided to return?"

"No, it's not what you think," Shireen insisted. "Actually, I don't know how to explain it to you. Everything is still so confusing to me. I don't want to depend upon this land. Everything here hurts me so much. Do you understand?"

"Of course. If I were in your place, I'd make the same decision."

"Doesn't it make you sad that I'm leaving?" suggested Shireen.

"It makes me sad that I thought there was something more between us," he acknowledged.

"Luqman, please don't think you were just a rebound relationship. But I don't know what's happened to me. It is as though I've suddenly realized I'm thirty years old. That life is slipping away from me, or spinning away to some other, inaccessible place. Do you understand? I don't want to end up as an old woman, alone and lonely in an empty house."

Luqman didn't respond, and his heart began to beat faster. Was this a life preserver she was throwing him just before he went under? Or—just the opposite—was she pronouncing a final sentence of death against him and informing him she couldn't revoke it?

Luqman said, "I hope you find a man who will make you happy. You deserve the best in life."

"You haven't asked me to stay. Don't you love me?"

"It's because I love you more than you imagine that I don't ask you to stay."

Luqman stood up, frowning. He announced to Shireen that he couldn't handle anymore discussion on this and had to go. Shireen followed him to the living room. She grabbed his hand and begged him to stay a little longer. He gave in and sat on the sofa. She sat down beside him.

We're ruined! That's what was running through his mind. And what an utter loss, Partner! Goddamn women! Deceitful, complicated, good for nothing! Look at Marina. She ended up in jail after falling in love with a drug dealer who had enticed her with marriage so he could put her to work. Salaam no longer had eyes for anything but Najeeb and his sadomasochistic sessions. As for Miss Shireen, she intended to travel to Paris alone because she suddenly discovered she was thirty!

A desert mirage, that what's you are! A scarecrow, a ghost, a dog, a nothing. You've been humiliated enough. Come on, Partner. Let's go back to our world. We'll disappear into it and never emerge until the day of resurrection. Forget Paris and your dream of escaping this absurd reality.

Goddamn this country! Destructive and murderous, it wraps you up like a spider's web, blocking you in as it squeezes. Death doesn't come all at once, but instead you are bled slowly, for years, for a lifetime. Goddamn this country, which only sides with the powerful and destroys the weak. Tyrannous, burning, with no limit to its harms. Killing, torturing, exterminating, and then marching in the funeral procession to demand retribution and insist on vengeance. If only the fire had consumed it! If only the flood had come over it, submerged it, and wiped it from the face of the earth, leaving no one behind to speak of what had been!

It's all the war's fault. If it hadn't ended, we wouldn't be ruined now, destined to beg and plead for the compassion of women. Certain people ignited the conflagration, and then they put it out, as though the war were a game. As though we were animals, stones, insects. And me? Us? How will we live now in this rabid age, the era of peace, decline, disgust, corruption, plunder, betrayal, lies, tricks, appearances—

"What are you thinking about?" Shireen interrupted.

Luqman sighed deeply. "Nothing. I'm thinking about this life here."

"I don't understand how you can stand it all. Don't you ever think about moving away?"

Luqman tensed up. "Even if that had occurred to me, do you think...In any case, how is it your problem? Just forget it. Let's talk about something else."

Shireen turned her head to look at the sea, biting her nails and thinking. After a few moments of silence, she said in a trembling voice, "Do you know there isn't a sea in Paris?"

Luqman turned to her, uncertain, and she went on, "The people there are cold, the loneliness is deadly, and the weather is bleak. I work all day, and I only come home in the evening. Do you think you could endure all that?"

Luqman answered her suddenly and hurriedly, "I would learn French, and I would look for work, and I would take care of you, and I would keep you warm, and I would wait for you not just for the day but for an entire life, Shireen. How could you think to ask me if I could endure life with the single person who has given my life meaning, and without whom I would rather die?"

"And we'll get married, and you'll give me children?" Shireen said.

She said it! She uttered it! She pronounced the words! We—will—get—married! Oh, God! What joy, what luck! What is wrong with you, Partner, that you are as lifeless as a prepubescent donkey? Come on, get up! Let's take Miss Shireen in our embrace, kiss her, and squeeze her between our arms.

CHAPTER 19

Luqman came to a stop in the house, thinking about what he should do now after having finished everything necessary. It was still too early for him to go to bed, and he was tense as he waited for the time to pass.

He went to the bedroom and brought out two suitcases. He set them in the entryway near the door. That was the last of his preparations for the following day. All he had left to do was take a shower, put on new clothes, drink his coffee, and call a taxi to take him to the airport.

Who would have believed a happy ending was coming after so much waiting and suffering, and that so many happy surprises would come his way, surpassing his wildest imagination? Here he was, having signed the marriage certificate with Shireen in the French embassy. She had gone ahead to Paris while he stayed behind to finish some paperwork and business transactions.

Tomorrow, we'll catch up with her, Partner, and we'll

bid farewell to this disgusting country and its mangy life. We've lost our fight in the civil war, yet we have won something much harder: the decisive campaign in our war with peace. If the war had continued full steam ahead, would you have gotten to know—or even dreamed of getting to know—Miss Shireen? You would have won power, money, and women as spoils, but on the other hand, you would have lost out on the name, the social status, and the Parisian future. What's more, would you have enjoyed with anyone else all the respect and prestige that your union with Shireen will bestow upon you?

From now on, Partner, I'll be called "Monsieur Luqman." And you and I, we'll get to know as many monsieurs and madames as hairs on my head or stars in the sky. Maybe I'll even trade in your cheap peasant's name after acquiring another citizenship, and I'll call you "Monsieur Alan," "Monsieur Patrick," or "Monsieur François."

Dear God! When will tomorrow come, when the airplane takes us up to the seventh heaven, and we never look back! We'll peel off our old, worn-out skin and be born anew as someone with no history, but just a future, like any newborn baby.

Luqman put his hand in his shirt pocket and took out his new passport. He opened it and looked closely at the visa stamp he had acquired that morning. He put it up to his nose to smell it. The ink was still fresh. And the date was clear, not open to any doubt.

When he had gotten back to the house, he had seen

the doorman and wished him a good morning, which he didn't usually do. He wasn't bothered by the doorman's weird accent or the racket his kids made, racing like rats through the different floors of the building. Why should he care ever again that the doorman resembled a security guard, a policeman, or a spy? Why should he care that the doorman had a weird accent, was arrogant, and was backed up by the state or the army? What did he care that there was a choking economic crisis, that the poor got poorer, that the roads were crowded, or that a sudden earthquake might wreak complete havoc and wipe out everything? What did it matter, as long as Luqman was leaving on a one-way ticket, heading out with the intention to never look back?

Indeed, Luqman was no longer part of this country, not since he married Shireen and became a legal French citizen with all the ensuing rights and obligations. The new Luqman no longer had a place in his heart for hatred or spite after being taken over by Miss Shireen—and by the fruits of the future riches she was preparing for him, which were dropping into his hands with only the slightest effort on his part. The Luqman who was traveling the next morning was a person as beautiful on the outside as his heart was pure on the inside. If he had wanted, he could even have shed a tear at the sight of a beautiful flower, a sparrow, or a small child.

You, too, Partner. You ought to repent your sins and forget the days of the Albino, Najeeb, and Salaam. Poor guys, they'll remain here, living in this giant trash can.

Neither the rats nor their prayers will save them. How will they explain your disappearance, and what might they say when they notice that you've left? For that matter, who knows what they are blaming right now for your having cut them off and stayed away so long?

Luqman felt a longing for Salaam's neighborhood. What if he went to visit her and passed the time with her as he waited for nightfall? That way, he would have seen her, her and Najeeb. He would have reassured them and satisfied his own conscience that he had done his duty towards them as a friend. He wouldn't tell them about his travel plans, of course, but maybe later on he would send them a postcard letting them know how things were going and how he had made it overseas.

Luqman grabbed his jacket from the hook, put it on, and took the elevator down. When he went out the front door of the building, the doorman called after him, "Goodbye, Mr. Luqman! I hope you know we are at your service, and that you won't hesitate to ask if there's anything you need."

Luqman thanked him, wished him a good evening, and went out smiling.

CHAPTER 20

The light was on inside, which is why Luqman kept knocking on the door. When he thought about leaving, it occurred to him to go up to Lurice's and look for Salaam there, but he changed his mind when he remembered that Salaam seldom left the house, even for a moment, without turning off the lights. What if he went around the house and tried to enter from the kitchen balcony?

He jumped over the low wall when he saw the kitchen door was open. He stopped, flabbergasted by the amount of dirty dishes piled up in the sink, the garbage strewn about the floor, and the remains of food. The place was crawling with rats and cockroaches. He called out to Salaam, then Najeeb, but there was no answer. In the end, he went inside and found her in the living room.

Salaam's hair was disheveled, and she looked like an entirely different person. She had lost a lot of weight. Her skin was pale, her eyes were sunken, and, dressed in a baggy nightgown spotted with grease, she seemed half the woman she used to be. He looked around at the chaos piling up on all sides. Her hands were playing with something, and from a distance, he tried to make out what was absorbing her so completely that she hadn't noticed his repeated knocking on the door or the fact that he was standing in front of her that very moment.

He greeted her, but she didn't respond. He addressed her again, but she didn't even lift her eyes. Instead, she went on, all her attention engrossed in what she was doing. Luqman came closer and saw she was pulling the small cotton pills from the fabric of her nightgown. She finally noticed him when he shook her. She looked up at him, perplexed, as though waiting for him to ask the question that made him tear her away from what she had been doing.

"Where's Najeeb?"

"What?"

"Salaam! I asked you where Najeeb is."

"Najeeb? He's sleeping."

Luqman left her and went to the bedroom. He opened the door and flipped the light switch, but it didn't turn on. He took a step inside. A vile odor struck his nostrils and was soon sticking in his throat. The odor penetrated to his stomach and turned it over violently before beginning to pull, as if to drag his insides out through his mouth.

He lifted the edge of his shirt to cover his nose. He took the lighter out of his pocket and ignited it. He saw

Najeeb stretched out on the bed. Najeeb's corpse had already begun decomposing. His face, his hands and feet, and his bloated belly were swimming in a yellow liquid mixed with excrement. His eyes were a pasture of worms.

Luqman ran to open the window. He leaned out, desperate for fresh air. He vomited everything in his intestines. He kept vomiting until he thought he would choke then and there, or that his eyes would pop out of their sockets. Finally, he rushed out of the room, heading for the bathroom. He scrubbed himself with soap and water to settle the nausea in his stomach and lungs.

Luqman went back to Salaam and found her just as she had been, bent over her lap, lost in the act of pulling elusive threads out of her cotton nightgown. Luqman sat nearby. He looked closely at her face, thinking about how to get through to her and draw her out in conversation. After a few moments of silence, he said, "I found Najeeb sleeping in his bed."

"Of course. It's better for us to let him sleep. He's very tired."

"What's the matter with him, Salaam?"

"He's sick! That's what the doctor told me: 'Your husband is very sick, Mrs. Salaam.' Do you hear that, Luqman? He thought Najeeb was my husband! But as long as he is resting well, I told him, he will recover and feel better."

"And how did the doctor know he was sick, Salaam?"

"What kind of question is that, Luqman? I was the one who sent for him, naturally!"

"I mean, why did you send for him if Najeeb was only complaining of a minor fatigue?"

"Minor fatigue? He was wasting away! He would spend all day, every day, in his laboratory, and I barely saw him. Recently, he began spending most of the night in there too. I kept telling him he would get sick if he kept on in that way, but he would just reply that he was testing a new method after his chemical experiments had failed, and that he was pursuing other ways that relied on biological warfare...If you had seen him, Luqman, you would have brought him to the hospital immediately and hooked up his IV yourself. The important thing is that on the night I left Saleem, after he decided to go live with his parents—"

"Najeeb decided to live with his parents?"

"No, Saleem!"

"Saleem? What's he doing here?"

"Just wait! I left Saleem underground with his parents. Then I came up to the house and prayed and went to sleep."

"You buried Saleem underground?"

"What are you talking about? Are you trying to drive me crazy, Luqman? I said I left him underground—in the cellar! Quit interrupting me, or I'll stop talking!"

"Fine, Salaam, go on. I won't interrupt you again."

"I said goodbye to Saleem, and I dozed off. But Najeeb began tossing and turning in his sleep. In the end, his cries woke me up. He had become delirious. I got up and felt his forehead, and I saw he was burning up.

I gave him the all medicine I had, and I started putting cold compresses on his forehead, hoping his temperature would go down. But it kept going up until it reached 104 degrees..."

Salaam lost her train of thought for a few moments. Luqman didn't say anything, waiting for her to continue. But she got up and moved away. He stopped her by asking where she was going.

"To make some coffee," she replied.

Luqman thanked her, insisting he didn't want anything, that he had eaten dinner and drunk a whole pot of coffee just before coming to see her.

Salaam smiled and sat down again. She said, "Here you are, coming to see me, Luqman, and I was meaning to call you."

"Why?"

"I want you to talk to Najeeb about me. I mean, I want you to ask him if he intends to marry me, or whether the thought has at least crossed his mind."

"No problem, Salaam. I promise I'll bring the matter up with him as soon as he gets better. But he's sick now, and we ought to get him better as soon as possible. Hey, you haven't told me whether the temperature came down afterwards."

"Of course. After appearing feeble and sick, without any strength to move, life suddenly came back to him, and once again he was irritable, nervous, tense, and he would get angry at the smallest things."

"He got better then?"

"No. The doctor said those were symptoms of the illness, and that Najeeb ought to get to the hospital right away."

"And what was the illness, Salaam?"

"So I pleaded with the doctor to leave him with me. I gave him money, and I swore that if he went on like that, I would take care of bringing him in myself. I was certain his condition was not serious and didn't call for notifying the authorities and the Ministry of Health."

"Notify them of what?"

"And then his eyes became bloodshot. After that, his tongued started swelling up, and recurring bouts of vomiting got him up several times a day. When I bribed the doctor, he had told me, 'I'll leave you alone for now and come back after five days.' That was the time he set for the illness to subside and for Najeeb to begin the road to recovery."

"And did the doctor come back?"

"Of course he did."

"And what did he do?"

"Nothing. I made him think I had gone and taken Najeeb to the clinic. I left him a note on the door, thanking him for everything that he had done, and letting him know that 'my husband' was recovering."

"And how long ago was that visit from the doctor, Salaam?"

"About two weeks."

"And why did you make him think Najeeb was getting better when he was still sick?"

"Because he claimed that Najeeb was afflicted! Because he was going to tell on him and put him in quarantine for forty days!"

"Afflicted with what, Salaam? With what?"

"'With what, Salaam, with what?'" Salaam mimicked. "With the plague, Luqman, the plague!" She burst into laughter.

Luqman could only jump up, aghast, feeling every hair on his body standing on end. He quickly edged away toward the door to get out of this polluted, contaminated place. She followed, hanging onto him and imploring him to stay until Najeeb woke up so he could talk to him about her and persuade him he had to marry her.

Luqman tried to get away by promising to return the following morning, no matter what. But she wouldn't let him go, wrapping her arms around him and clinging to him even as he tried to keep her away. When she started getting aggressive, he pushed her so hard that she fell to the floor. He shot like an arrow out of the apartment, not turning aside for anything.

CHAPTER 21

He didn't know what made him do it, or why it even occurred to him in the first place.

He had gotten halfway home when he stopped for a moment. He, who still couldn't believe he had escaped Salaam's clutches, decided to go back. Perhaps it was the memory of the Albino, or else his desire to say goodbye and be rid of his memory...Actually, it was Lurice's money that brought him back, the cash that would go to waste after Najeeb had died and Salaam had gone crazy. Salaam would definitely meet his same fate, death by the plague.

He went up the stairs slowly, taking pains to avoid any noise that would give him away. He stopped and strained his ears to listen. There was nothing at all. He thought Lurice must be asleep or had passed on to the next world. That's actually what seemed most likely to Luqman. He had turned around to go back out when he heard the sound of a key turn once in the lock, then a second time.

After that, complete silence.

Luqman didn't understand. He paused for a few moments at the top of the stairs, watching the door and waiting for her to open it. It didn't open, nor did she come out or make any sign. He got closer and reached out to grasp the handle. He turned it slowly to confirm the door was still locked and that he had just imagined it all.

But the door opened. It let out a slow creak and came to a stop. Luqman put his eye in the gap to steal a glance inside. Everything was very dark and still, but it occurred to him that Lurice must have supposed her visitor was just Salaam.

Luqman stepped over the threshold with a sense of apprehension, but not fear. When the door swung shut behind him, he felt a solid, heavy object crash into the back of his head.

He couldn't say how much time passed before he awoke. He didn't see her. He discovered he was lying on the floor, his mouth was muffled, and his hands and feet were bound with various scraps of cloth.

Luqman strained at the bonds on his hands, trying to get free. They were tied too tight, and he couldn't break them. He started moving like a snake and wriggled along until he reached the wall. He planted his feet on the floor and pushed until his upper half was vertical and he could sit with his back against the wall.

He caught the muffled rustle of steps before Lurice came into view. She didn't pay him any attention. She just passed through the room as though she didn't notice him, as though he weren't there, disappearing again into the opposite room, the door of which opened onto wherever he was. He heard her closing windows and dragging a heavy metal object on the floor. Then she opened a faucet, and he guessed she was in the kitchen. Perhaps she had been thirsty, and now she was getting something to drink.

Luqman looked around, trying to figure out something of his surroundings. He wasn't able to see through the wall of darkness that lay heavy on his eyelids. He heard the clatter of a car slowly coming closer until it stopped nearby. Its lights reflected up to where he was, illuminating a few details.

His eyes darted around quickly, trying to absorb as much information as possible. He learned he was in the living room. He saw a sewing machine crouched in one of the corners. Around it were rolls of fabric, papers, and scraps of cloth strewn upon the floor. He turned to his left, and he noticed a rope fixed between the facing walls, upon which she had hung a number of things. He stared hard, and it became clear that it was children's clothing since there came into view the outlines of pants legs and sleeves attached by clothes hooks and floating in midair.

She just had to look at him to see he wasn't a stranger, come secretly to rob or assault her. I'm Luqman, Mrs. Lurice, he would say to her, the friend of your only son, the Albino. He would be out of there in a few moments. After just a few moments, she would remember he was there, or he would remind her, and she would untie his hands and let him go back home. And from there to the airport.

God! What was it that made him to go back to her? Was a handful of dollars worth suffering what he was going through now? Oh, well. Just wait a little, Luqman, and things will come out alright, God willing. What can a weak, old woman like Lurice do to you, and why should you be afraid of her? Is she going to kill you? Of course not! The worst-case scenario is that she keeps you here and makes you miss your flight. So be it. You'll take a different flight the day after tomorrow and let Shireen know you've exchanged the ticket for some reason.

He swore to God he wasn't going to lay a finger on her. He'd even forget the matter of her money if she let him go in one piece. But how could he make her understand when she had gagged him, which prevented him from speaking to her and persuading her of his good intentions?

Lurice came back to him. She went over to shut the window. Then she went to the balcony door and closed it. She did the same with the other doors leading into that room, with the exception of the kitchen door, which she left open. She came over to Luqman and bent down to get a closer look. She smiled at him and caressed his face tenderly. He felt reassured, believing she would free him. But she sat down on the floor next to him, leaning her back against the wall. Then she reached over and patted his bound hands, keeping them between hers and pulling them towards her.

"Do you know, Elias, it is the Lord who gave you to me. He came to me at night in a dream and said to me, 'Stop crying, Lurice! Your breast, which for so long you have laid bare and beaten with your two clenched fists, has pained me. You will have a child soon. In a few weeks, you will be pregnant.' And so it was. When you were born, your father cried for days. And when he died, I didn't cry for him. I said, 'The house still has someone to protect it, and I still have a man: my son, Elias.'

"How did you get away from me? I do not know. How did you grow up so fast and become a different person, someone called 'the Albino,' who didn't spring from my loins or your father's? God! When I saw you that night, I wished death had taken me and delivered me from that moment, which destroyed me and transformed my life into long years of torture!

"I came straight back home, not turning aside for anything. My heart nearly dropped out of me into the street, and my lungs were choking with the memory of what I had seen you doing. I cried the entire night. I prayed on my knees, asking the Lord to inspire me with what I ought to do to absolve you and redeem your sins. He didn't answer me. I said I wasn't strong enough to go on living after that. I said I would die so as no longer to see what was torturing my conscience, separating me from you and making me feel you weren't my son, but rather an evil stranger who had sold his depraved soul to the devil!

"But a voice spoke to me. I wasn't sleeping or dreaming, but wide-awake, with my eyes open. I started praying and asking forgiveness for you and for me, but the voice said, 'What's wrong, Lurice, and why do you keep beseeching me in tears?'

"I told him about you. I described how I had gone to find you one evening when I hadn't seen you for days, and I was overcome with worry. I was afraid something bad had happened to you, you had become sick and bedridden, or a sniper's bullet had gotten you, or a bombardment or an explosion.

"I asked about the building you and your friends had confiscated and converted into your apartments and an office for distributing food. I made my way there, and I thought it strange how you were staying in that deserted, desolate place, which was still unfinished and had no trace of inhabitants. I went up the stairs slowly. On each floor I came to, I looked into the facing apartments and saw they were abandoned and shabby, without any doors. Then a sound of laughter, which I could tell was yours, reached my ears. My heart was reassured, and I said, 'I'll turn around and go back where I came from. I don't want to disturb him. I'll let him enjoy his evening with friends.

"If only that laugh hadn't suddenly been mixed with a scream! My heart fell. I turned around quickly and ran up the steps until I heard your laugh again, clear and sustained, ringing in my ears. I said, 'They're just playing a game.' I said you were playing with your friends and joking around with some sick, offensive joke. Then I got there. The broken door opened onto a long hallway. The long hallway led to a bathroom.

"I saw you...You were laughing! Why were you laughing, my son, when the man in front of you was naked, crying, pleading, wailing, screaming, and begging that you have mercy on his children, if there wasn't any mercy in your heart for him? Why were you laughing, Albino, when you were ripping out his fingernails with pliers and breaking his teeth with an iron ball, then pouring water on him and branding him with a red hot bar?

"I ran down the stairs. I was crying, not out of pity for your victim, but out of fear of you, of that face I saw on you, the face of a criminal, a tyrant, a beast, a monster. I wanted to slice off the breast with which I had nursed you, to amputate the arms that rocked you, to tear out the womb that bore you, and to cut off the tongue that had prayed to God for you, with the result that your body grew and got big and acquired all your cruelty and depravity.

"I told all this to the voice that addressed me. Then I asked it to take me, so that I might die and have some rest. And do you know what it answered me? 'Your little one, Elias, is being tormented, Lurice. It's the Albino who has taken him over.'

"And so it was. I killed you, Albino, in order to bring back my little Elias. I prepared dinner for you. You ate it and got up to go sleep in your room. I waited until I heard the sound of your light, regular snoring. I brought the gas canister in and opened it. Then I closed the door on you...

"But you kept coming to me at night, blaming me and

reproaching me. Then the reproaches turned to harsh re-bukes, and the rebukes to a torment of blows and threats of strangling. Perhaps it was because you died suddenly when you weren't expecting it. So here I am today, doing it with your full knowledge. Here I am, telling you I've closed all the windows, and I've opened the valve on the gas canister so that death will come to you slowly, like a sleep.

"It's good you came to me tonight because I was waiting for you. This time, I was ready for you, and I hid behind the door. I waited, my heart pounding. I was beg-ging the Lord He would inspire you to come in...and you did!"

CHAPTER 22

For a long time, the clouds had been coming to a halt,
piling up, uncertain, above that city.

One cloud asked its sister, "Don't you see the ground
trembling and shuddering underneath us?"

A second answered, "Yes! Indeed, these are the first
violent tremors of a devastating earthquake."

A third said, "In that case, let's move on. We've seen
enough here."

So the clouds gathered together quickly and made
ready to leave. They looked down in farewell. Then they
exploded in tears.